Winona,

Thanks Again!
I hope you enjoy it.
Eric Reuben

WHERE MAN AND MONSTER MEET

Author: Eric Tamburino
Illustrated by: Chantal Tamburino
ISBN: 9781731484017
Independently Published

Contact:
wheremanandmonstermeet@gmail.com
https://wheremanandmonstermeet.com

Dedication:
To my mother who told me to write things down
and to my father who drove me to do it.

THE TABLE OF CONTENTS

THE CITY OF THE LOST

1

Everybody wore a mask in the city of Perditus. They wore masks of all different shapes and sizes. The rich had theirs forged from gold and silver; the common folk crafted theirs in iron or wood. A poor man's mask was made of fabric. Some masks covered the whole of the face, whereas others covered only half. All were decorated with intricate designs and paintings. In this city, your mask was your face: designed to express who you wished to be, but very rarely who you actually were. No one knows why this became the way of life, but everyone followed it as if it were an unspoken law. In fact, it was as if they were not even aware that they were wearing masks.

Matthias smiled as he slid his mask over his face and gently brushed back the musty stage curtain with his forefinger. The air seemed to fill with energy as more people crammed into the already congested theatre. Dust and sweat rose as men and women shuffled across the dirt floor, trying to create more room. Renegade children wove between adults, looking to get closer to the aged and faded wooden stage. Candles lining the stage emitted an almost mystical essence, permitting enough light for one to see the cracks in the walls. They rose up to the decrepit ceiling like veins in a man's skin.

Matthias did not flinch as the curtain fell back into place. His father, who managed the stage, had always reprimanded him for peeking out at the audience; however, after many years of stage life, he had perfected the motion, and from the outside it appeared as though the curtain had swayed ever so slightly. He took his place at the center of the stage, watching as his fellow performers followed suit. Confident in his abilities to perform, Matthias felt no fear as the curtain opened and he gazed into the faceless audience. This was the theatre of Perditus.

Following the conclusion of the play, Matthias returned to the tiny closet the performers called a dressing room. He wanted to switch out his mask. Most theatre masks only covered the top half of the face, leaving the mouth exposed for better expression and vocal projection. He reached up and removed it, placing it down on the shelf with a profound reverence. He smoothed back his hair before reaching for another.

The light but sturdy wood covered his full face and had a permanent unflinching smile carved into it. This mask had become his favorite because it portrayed him as happy, allowing him to feel relaxed and less like a performer. Tonight he felt more than happy; he had just made it to what very well could be the top of his career.

Matthias placed the mask over his face and, after tying the strings tightly, left, hoping to see what remained of the crowd in front of the theatre.

Matthias stood on the large stone steps of the theatre alongside his fellow performers, attentive to the praise of the people. He listened as they congratulated him. Then, moving past him, they shook hands with his father, promising to return again. Some wore familiar faces, others he noticed were new. He scanned the crowd with pleasure, until he came upon a figure who intrigued him.

The mask captured his attention, because for a moment

it looked as though the figure did not wear one. Her hair appeared smooth as silk, cascading over her bare shoulders in loose waves. She wore a full face mask, pale with perfectly defined features. It portrayed its expression through subtle detail, and added an air of mystery to this woman by giving the appearance that she held a secret. The mask did not appear to be happy or sad but rather, pleased. She wore a purple dress with an empire waist and a white silk belt. The hem touched the cobblestone and flowed from her body like an ocean tide. She stared right back at him. Matthias wanted to go to her but feared that if he took his eyes off of her and stepped out into the mass of people, he would lose her. Instead, he remained still, admiring her from afar.

A question drew Matthias back to the moment.

"Isn't that right, Matthias?"

He turned to his fellow performer, not knowing what the question had been.

"What? Yes, of course," Matthias responded, looking back toward the mysterious woman, only to find she had vanished. He bounded off of the steps and into the crowd and began searching a world of faceless people, though he did not entirely know why. He had no concept of what he would say to her if he found her, but he somehow knew that she would change his life. He pushed through the crowd until he reached the spot where she had been standing before she had slipped away. He grabbed the shoulders of passersby asking if anyone had seen her. Some became angry, others did not care, but none of them knew of the young woman he sought. As the street began to clear he had no choice but to abandon his search. She had eluded him.

He turned to walk back towards the theatre, and he saw her. He stared at her as a hunter spots a doe, careful not to startle her away. He approached, asking just above a whisper, "What is your name, my lady?"

"Anastasia," she said.

"Has anyone ever told you how beautiful you are, Anastasia?" he asked.

"Has anyone ever told you how forward you are...?"

"Matthias," he said, completing her question. "May I have the honor of walking you home? I hear the city can be quite perilous at night."

"You may," she replied. "But only halfway."

"Why is that?"

"Only halfway," she repeated.

Matthias agreed, and together they began to walk through the darkening city. He watched her out of the corner of his eye. She walked with a subtle confidence, not proud like an actress but not shuffling like most common folk. She did not appear to be anxious or nervous, just quiet, waiting with patience for him to initiate the conversation.

"Do you come to the theatre often? I have not seen you before," he asked.

"Now and then." All of her movements seemed to hold a practiced grace.

"Have you ever considered being an actress?"

Anastasia laughed.

"I don't know how you do it," she said, "getting on stage and baring your soul to all the world."

"Not exactly," he countered. "It's more like baring someone else's. I don't write the words, I just perform them."

"It still seems rather vulnerable."

"It can be."

"What was the hardest role you ever had to perform?" she asked.

Matthias thought for a moment.

"It's from a story called *The Seed*," he answered. "It's about an unhappy town and a young man who brings seeds to it. Some people want the seeds, others don't. But he is so sure

4

they will bring joy to the community. At the end of the story, it turns out he is a god bringing joy to the earth."

"Who did you play?" she asked.

"The god," he answered.

"Why was that role the hardest?"

"I don't know," he said. "I think it's hard to play someone so clear on what they want."

"Do you think only the gods have clarity?" she asked, with interest.

"I don't know," he answered as they both slowed to a stop.

They stood at an intersection everyone referred to as Market Square. Matthias knew it well and had performed here on several occasions.

"This is where we must part company," she said.

Matthias stopped, annoyed their time had come to a close. He had not asked half of the questions he had wanted to. She maintained her air of mystery in spite of her charm and wit. He had unintentionally talked about himself too much, and he knew he had to see her again.

"Thank you for the pleasure. I had a wonderful time," he said.

"I did as well," she replied.

"Perhaps we could do this again?"

"Maybe," she answered.

"I can live with that."

A week passed, and Anastasia had not returned. As he fell asleep each night, Matthias thought of her, replaying their time together over and over in his mind. So many questions for her and no answers. She had manipulated the conversation and let him do most of the talking. Matthias got the sense she was the type of person you could talk to for hours and walk away having gotten no deeper than the surface. He had been right, she would have made a fine actress. He fell asleep most nights begging the universe for one more chance to be with her, that he might fix his mistakes.

In the meantime, Matthias threw himself into his work. Performance after performance he did his best, hoping that she would be watching. He watched for her as people left the theatre, their praise meaning nothing to him anymore. After their final performance of the show, his friends invited him out to celebrate; but he declined the invitation. He remained at the theatre, locking the doors. He turned from the doors, and there she stood: his lady, gracing him with her presence.

"You were magnificent tonight," she complimented him.

"Thank you, but not half as magnificent as you," he countered with a low bow.

"I hear the city can be quite perilous at night," she teased.

"May I?" he asked, extending his hand in her direction.

"You may," she answered, "but only halfway."

They began to walk through the quiet streets of Perditus once more.

"So what do you-" she began.

"Oh, no," he interrupted, "I did all the talking last time, and I want to know more about you."

"Okay. What do you want to know?" she asked, with a mischievous grin.

"Why I can only walk you halfway home would be a good start."

"What's life without a little mystery?" she countered. "Start smaller."

"Hhhmm," Matthias thought. "What are your interests outside of the theatre?"

"Travel," she answered. "I love to see other places and hear their stories."

"Where have you traveled to?"

"Nowhere yet," she admitted. "But I have read many

histories, and I find so many of them fascinating."

"If you could travel anywhere, where would you go?" he asked.

"Everywhere," she said slowing to a stop. "Last question."

Matthias tried to make it seem as though he was thinking hard, but he had known what his last question would be since before the walk had begun.

"Would you get dinner with me next time, before I walk you home?" he asked, afraid it had come out too quickly.

"How do you know there will be a next time?" she asked.

"If I told you it would ruin the mystery. And after all," he paused for dramatic effect, "what's life without a little mystery?"

"Careful," she warned, and she leaned in to hug him.

Matthias felt flooded with euphoria as she slipped her arms around him. He could smell the perfume in her hair and he wondered if this was how it felt to be intoxicated. Then, just before she pulled away, she whispered;

"If you keep stealing my lines, I may just change my mind."

Week after week Anastasia came to the theatre for the last performance of each play. They would often get dinner, but Matthias always accompanied her to the spot halfway between the theatre and her home and say good night. Sometimes she would let him take her hand as they walked; other times she would not. But every time he walked her to that spot, she would thank him, embrace him, and whisper "goodnight." Matthias lived for those moments, where he could be so close to the young woman who kept herself so distant.

It was during this moment on no particular night he whispered to her.

"Please. Please, don't make me leave you here again."

She pulled away from his embrace, staring at him. He knew the next moments would decide everything. Then in silence, she took his hand and began to walk again. The silence remained with them, but Matthias welcomed it. Speech had not only been his gift in life but also his curse. He had made a name for himself at the theatre, but every actor knew, whether on or off the stage, that unrehearsed lines were far more dangerous to speak. Afraid to upset Anastasia or change her mind, he found silence to be his greatest companion for this trip. She continued to lead him through the darkest parts of the city. Candles had been extinguished, beggars were in the alleys, and people with far more nefarious intentions skulked in the shadows.

"This is a dangerous road. How could you let me leave you all those times? I should've been there with you."

"It's all right. You didn't know," she answered, squeezing his hand.

They approached the city gate, which had been shut for the evening. She smiled and waved to the guard, who returned a wave before opening the wicket.

Anastasia continued to lead Matthias out of the city and into the woods. Deeper and deeper they traveled, until they came upon a cottage. Matthias felt humbled when he saw the place. The untrimmed bushes had begun to grow up the sides of the rather tiny structure, consuming it. A dilapidated wicker bench decorated the front lawn. A dim light leaked from under the door. Matthias wondered if the unkempt little house would look better in the daylight or if it always looked like a witch's den. He tried to imagine it in its original state. It would have been small, the colors vibrant, the bushes trimmed, with a beautiful bench for her mother and father to sit on in nice weather. Matthias kept all these thoughts to himself, and tried to expel them from his mind as they approached the door. At times like these he realized just how grateful he was for his mask.

"It's late. Would you like to come in and have something to eat?" Anastasia asked.

Matthias agreed, worried it would be impolite to decline the invitation. Anastasia pushed open the door and led Matthias into the house. The temperature shifted from a permeating cold damp to a dry warmth which seemed to blanket his body. A large fire burning in the hearth provided heat, and the aroma of freshly cooked stew enveloped him. The interior proved to be much more inviting than the foreboding exterior.

A vast assortment of candles provided light to each room. Masks of deceased relatives hung upon the far wall, going back for generations. Handmade cushions and pillows with intricate designs lay upon each chair, and tiny trinkets and figurines were scattered about the house, many far too exotic for Matthias to recognize. Cluttered but cozy, he felt as though he were wading into a lifetime of memories, or perhaps several lifetimes, as he entered the house.

"Grandma," Anastasia called, slipping out of her shoes. She disappeared into a back room, leaving Matthias by the entryway. He waited, unsure of what to do. A few moments passed before Anastasia returned with her grandmother. Matthias stared in disbelief as he realized her grandmother did not wear a mask.

"And who is this young man?" her grandmother asked, with a hint of girlish charm.

"His name is Matthias, Grandma," Anastasia said.

"It is very nice to meet you, Matthias," her grandmother said. "Would you like to have supper with us?"

Matthias's first inclination was to leave as quickly and politely as he could, but a seed of curiosity began to sprout in his mind. He could leave, or he could stay and possibly learn the story of this strange woman who did not wear a mask.

After a moment's reflection he realized the invitation had not been so much a question as it was an insistence. His own grandmother had never permitted him to leave until he had eaten something.

"That would be lovely," he responded.

Over the course of dinner, there were many questions, many answers, and much laughing. Anastasia's grandmother proved a pleasant conversationalist and more or less normal, in spite of the fact that she wore no mask. She told Matthias about her travels as a seamstress when she was young, collecting fine fabrics and making them into beautiful dresses. He listened while she told of her many great adventures, glancing over at Anastasia from time to time. It was clear Anastasia had heard the stories many times, but she did not seem weary of them. Her grandmother possessed a painful honesty, which Matthias found to be refreshing. By the time dinner ended, Matthias judged it would be permissible to ask the final obvious question, which still lingered.

"May I be blunt?" he asked.

"Yes," her grandmother replied.

"Why do you not wear a mask?"

"I wore a mask for many years, never truly feeling comfortable with it. So I began to ask myself why I wore it. Why I needed it. I realized I didn't want to wear a mask all my life. I wanted to look at my reflection and see my face, not a mask. So, I removed it," she finished with a smile.

"She even burned it," Anastasia added.

Matthias thought about this for a moment. *She must be crazy! Not just to take off her mask, but to burn it!*

"When did this happen?"

"It happened late in my life, I'm sorry to say. I wish I had done it sooner," she responded.

Matthias turned to see Anastasia. *Has she taken off her mask?* he wondered.

Anastasia's grandmother seemed to read his thoughts. "It is up to the wearer to discern why he or she wears the mask. No one can take off another's, and very few choose to look beneath their own."

At the end of supper, Matthias bid them both goodnight. Her grandmother assured him that he would be welcome any time. Anastasia offered to walk him to the edge of the wood, but he declined, telling her he remembered the way. He walked home in silence, reviewing the evening's events in his mind.

As if he had been pricked by a needle with a slow-killing poison, the conversations of that night spread through Matthias, until questions began to manifest in his mind like voices screaming. Night after night he took the stage, losing his heart and soul to each character, each line, each emotion. Baring himself, digging deeper and deeper, until like molten gold, he would either purify or dissolve with his imperfections. He changed his mask with every role, all the while wondering, *Who have I become? Who am I beneath this?*

The theatre housed the only mirror in the city; it was used as a set piece, but only when absolutely necessary. It offered Matthias no comfort as he stared, wondering what he would see if he removed his mask. He let his fingers trace every edge and crevice of his wooden facepiece. *What lies beneath this inhuman thing? Why am I so adamant to leave it on?* He could find any character in the mirror, but never himself.

But the questions Anastasia's grandmother had seemed to slip into Matthias's mind were not the only change for Matthias. His prestige began to rise within the troupe with each role he took, until he became the talk of the city. People traveled great distances to see him, and in time rumors began to spread that he had become the greatest actor in the region. In spite of all of his success, he lay awake at night, haunted by the questions which had taken root within his mind. It almost seemed the more his fame grew, the more lost he felt.

Matthias and Anastasia walked through the cobbled streets hand-in-hand, as had become their tradition, watching the dim lights of each house go out. It was late, and although Matthias was exhausted, he refused to be anything less than a gentleman and had insisted on walking Anastasia home. His father had added two extra performances of the past show, and though it had been lucrative, Matthias had felt distracted.

He had not stopped thinking of Anastasia. Over and over he tried to sift the sandstorm of feelings he had for her, until another riddle had begun to demand his attention. How did she feel about him?

After the visit with her grandmother, Anastasia had continued to visit the theatre, and Matthias had begun to spend more time with her. Most days they could only afford brief walks in the city, but occasionally they found the time to walk around the fields beyond the city walls. They would pack bread and cheese and spend the afternoon sitting on one of Anastasia's grandmother's quilts. Being with her had become the only thing he found himself longing for besides the stage.

Matthias stopped as they neared the edge of the forest, and he turned to face her.

"I can't stop thinking about you," he said.

"I can't stop thinking about you either, and I don't want to," she said, taking his hands in hers.

His thoughts began to race, and the pounding of his heart distracted him. He had heard those words so many times before; but it had always been in the theatre, never real. Those words had never been for him. He knew what would come next, but he still was not prepared.

"I love you," she said.

Matthias stared into her eyes as the two stood encased in silence. He cared very deeply for Anastasia, but there was so much he didn't know. Did he love her, or was that simply another mask? Matthias struggled for words, but nothing came. He wanted to say them back to her. He wanted to mean them. He wanted to know with all certainty, but he didn't.

"I can't-" he began to croak, before she hushed him.

Again, silence.

"Anastasia, why do you wear your mask?" he asked, trying to change the subject.

Anastasia looked away, uncomfortable. She crossed her arms and lowered her gaze, trying to figure out where to begin.

Matthias second-guessed his question. "I'm sorry. You don't need to-"

She shook her head, silencing him. "She's not my grandmother..."

Matthias cocked his head in surprise.

"She is not my grandmother," she repeated fighting to quell her emotions. "My parents left me as a baby on the side of the road, with no explanation as to who I was or how I had come to be left there. Grandma told me that a traveler found me. Not equipped to deal with a baby, he carried me until he met my grandma, then he passed me off to her, a complete stranger..."

Her emotions, which she had tried so hard to stave off, won, and she began to weep.

Matthias knew he would never forgive himself for bringing such a deep pain back to the surface. He had not expected it. How could he have known? He placed a hand on her shoulder.

She collected herself and continued.

"As a baby, I had no mask and was passed along from one person to the next. I wear my mask because I am afraid..." she choked through tears, "I am afraid that underneath... I am unlovable."

Matthias wanted to embrace her, to hold her close and comfort her, but she stepped away.

Nothing I do can ever heal these wounds.

They continued on in silence, her hand withdrawn from his. He wished she would say something. He didn't dare speak another word. As they came to the house, she picked up her pace and left him without a word.

Relief swept over Matthias when Anastasia returned to the theatre as usual. It was the last performance of this play, and he had been afraid she would not be there. His head had been a whirlwind of emotion since she had left him outside of her house, and he was sure hers was as well. He had replayed his words to her and her words to him over and over in whispers as if he had been rehearsing a new play where the main character thought he was two different people. He had been a fool. He never should have asked her. Not only had he still not solved the mystery of his feelings for Anastasia, or the greater question of the mask, but now he found himself haunted by the image of a baby on the side of the road, unattended, and it tore at his soul. He could not even fathom what she must feel.

After the performance Matthias could not wait to see Anastasia. He did not want to receive praise or lock up the theatre once everyone one had left; but he did it just the same, shaking hands and exchanging pleasantries with his patrons. All the while he watched her from the corner of his eye. She stood waiting for him at the bottom of the stone stairs next to the column. She had stood there the night he had first laid eyes on her, and she was still just as enchanting. She was perfect.

He would apologize to her and beg her forgiveness. No, he had said enough; he would wait for her to speak. An apology would only refresh the memory. He would wait for her to speak, and he would keep the conversation plain and superficial.

After the last person had left, Matthias shut the theatre doors and locked them. He turned to Anastasia and descended the steps.

"Hello," she said, her voice like a song.

"Hello," he answered, once more debating if he should apologize.

Anastasia took him by the hand and pulled him close.

"Walk me home," she said, and they began to walk just as they always did, hand in hand. Neither spoke. They enjoyed the company of the other and the music the night provided. Their feet tapped the cobblestone, and in the distance several drunken men could be heard singing an old dirge. The city was dark, but the clear night sky offered the guiding light of the moon and a million stars. Matthias noticed none of these things. He focused on Anastasia, the warmth of her hand in his.

They passed through the city gate, waved to the guard, and began their journey into the woods. Matthias knew the way, but tonight Anastasia led him somewhere new. She branched off of the main path and brought him to a clearing. It was a small paradise hidden within the thick wood.

A small pond lay under the sad gaze of a weeping willow. A mild breeze rose and fell, swaying the branches and making it seem as if the tree were dancing to a slow, romantic song. A tiny river poured steadily into the pond on one side and flowed out from the other. The gentle trickle of water over stone met Matthias's ears as they walked through the grass deeper into the clearing. Hundreds of fireflies began to rise and float around them like tiny glowing snowflakes. Anastasia lay in the grass by the pond and motioned for Matthias to do

15

the same. She reached for his arm and placed it around her. Then they lay there in silence looking out into the night sky.

"Why do you wear the mask, Matthias?" Anastasia asked.

The question caught Matthias off guard. They had lain in silence long enough to watch the moon cross the better half of the sky. It was unlike her to initiate such a deep conversation. Matthias chuckled as he began to piece together his answer. "I have been asking myself that for weeks now. I am not sure why. I grew up in theatre. I guess I just like them. I feel like the people I pretend to be: brave warriors and heroes, amusing servants, or crafty villains." As he spoke his mind carried him down the stream of his thought process, and when Matthias reached the end he began to see the answer.

Anastasia knew as his voice trailed off. She reached over and took his hand.

"I wear the mask," he continued, "because it is all I've known. When I landed my first role in the theatre, my father was so proud of me, everyone was. As I performed time after time, the praise never ceased. Deep down though, I am not a hero or a comedian like the great ancient men I pretend to be. I wear the mask because if I take it off… it is quite possible there is nothing worth seeing underneath."

Anastasia looked into his eyes. "You have never seen your own face?"

"No," he said, toying with her fingers in his hands. "Have you?" He knew what her answer would be.

She looked away, but he could hear her smile in her voice.

"I have. I thought about what I told you about my past and my fears, but I also thought about how happy my grandmother is, to be herself. So I went to the pond and, looking at my reflection in the water, took off my mask…"

"What did you see?"

"Myself!" she exclaimed. "Look!"

She reached up and slid off her mask. Matthias took one look at her and knew that he would be forever plagued by a new question. *How could anyone leave her on the side of the road?*

"Has anyone told you how beautiful you are?" he asked her, as he did when they had first met.

"Only you," she smiled shyly, and Matthias felt his soul move in a way it had not been moved before. "Matthias, would you kiss me?"

He pulled her close and leaned in until their foreheads touched.

"You have to take off your mask," she whispered.

Matthias reached up but, as soon as his fingers touched it, he froze. It had become so comfortable, so familiar, the thought of removing it seemed unthinkable.

"I don't know what's underneath; I don't know that I can."

"I will love you no matter what is behind your mask. I promise," she pleaded, taking his hands and kissing them gently. He wondered how it would feel to let her lips touch his. He slid his hands out of hers. "I am sorry," he struggled with the words, "but I can't take it off...not even for you."

"Why are you so afraid to let me see who you really are underneath?"

"Because I don't know who I am underneath."

"Will you ever?"

"I don't know."

Anastasia cradled herself. Matthias reached for her, but she pulled away.

"I don't know that I can live with that," she stated.

Matthias realized he was going to lose her, and in the same moment he realized he didn't want to. He spoke and the words surprised even himself.

"Anastasia, please, we loved each other in spite of our

masks. Can't we just continue as we were?"

He picked up her mask off of the ground, extending it to her.

"I would be lying," she said in sorrow.

Matthias watched as a tear rolled down her cheek and he felt his heart begin to break.

She wiped the tear away and pulled his face close, kissing the cheek of his mask.

"Goodbye, Matthias," she whispered, and she left him.

Anguish would be too mild an emotion to describe Matthias's state. His heart ached for Anastasia, but she never returned. Months came and passed, and an anger began to take root and spread through his soul. He hated himself for his weakness, his fear, and yet even now he could not bring himself to remove his mask. He tried to forget her, but after each performance he still caught himself watching the steps of the theatre. The seasons changed and the snow began to fall. One cold winter's night, Matthias found himself in the woods, returning to Anastasia's house only to find out that she had left for a far-off region to sell quilts her grandma had made. He almost did not return to the city that night.

After each performance, he began to go with his troupe to their favorite tavern. The stage was the only place he could forget Anastasia, and so when he was not on stage he needed a distraction. They would eat, drink, and sing the songs of old. Due to his rising fame, he found himself never wanting for a conversation. It took effort at first, but it became easier for him to lose himself in it all. However, it was not enough, and he would become aloof, staring into an empty glass as if it were a wishing well. It was on one night such as this that his father interrupted his thoughts by slamming a fresh pint down on the table.

"What's wrong?" his father asked him as he pushed the pint over towards his son. "You've done very well these past few months. Everybody loved your performances; you're a sensation! What is wrong?"

Matthias stared into the mug at his dark reflection. "Do you ever wonder who we are beneath these masks?"

The man looked at his son and laughed. "Well, look at you, trying to take on the big questions!" Matthias bowed his head in shame as his father took another swig of his pint.

"Son, let me tell you something. It doesn't matter! This is what matters," he said, holding up a small purse of coins. "Because this," he said pointing to the pouch, "provides this," he finished, waving his hand dramatically at the barroom.

His father was right. What did it matter? He had become so many people, who cared who he actually was? He was an actor. Famous. Successful.

He was disgusted with himself.

Matthias sat with his friends for a bit longer before he excused himself for the night. He began walking aimlessly down streets and alleys until he found himself on the wall of the main gate of the city, overlooking the forest in which Anastasia had lived. *Where is she?* he wondered. He remembered their conversations and how they had first met. Her beautiful face he had seen only once but would never forget. He remembered the pain in her eyes. He reached up and let his fingers trace the smile carved into his mask.

"You look like a young man with a lot on his mind," said a voice.

Matthias turned to see an older gentleman standing to his left. The man kept his face hidden in the shadows, and Matthias could not make out his mask. He hadn't heard the man approach.

A voice on his right said, "It helps to talk sometimes."

He turned to see a young boy sitting on the edge of the

wall next to him. The child did not wear a mask. Matthias, unsure how either character had gotten there or how to proceed, tried to avoid the invitation.

"No one seems to want to hear about it," Matthias countered.

The older gentleman continued to face the horizon. "I have traveled this earth for a long time and seen many things. Tell me what's on your mind, and I may ease the burden for a while."

Matthias shrugged. "There is this girl…"

"There always is," chuckled the older man.

"And she left me, because she wanted me to take off my mask but I would not."

Matthias watched the old man flinch as he said this.

"To fully open yourself up to someone is dangerous. It's very easy to get hurt," the older man commented.

Matthias decided to continue. "She took off her mask. She let me see her face. She opened herself to me, and I betrayed that. I have begun to wonder why we wear masks at all."

"These are not safe thoughts," the older man insisted. "You shouldn't be thinking them."

The little boy spoke again. "Why do you wear your mask?"

Matthias looked at him. He seemed so innocent, so genuine. "Because I am afraid of what is underneath."

"Why?" the child asked, turning to face him. "It is only you underneath."

"Because sometimes you can be very ugly, weak, or broken," the man answered for Matthias. "A mask is safe. It protects us from others and ourselves. You are but a boy; you would not understand." The man reached into his bag and took out a mask. He handed it to Matthias. "This will protect you."

Matthias took it in his hands, examining the unidentifiable

material from which it had been created. It seemed more a helmet than a mask. It had no face.

"I don't understand. Shouldn't a mask portray how you wish to appear? This has no face at all."

"Exactly," the man said, excitement in his voice. "It's perfect. It adapts. It is a magic mask. You never have to take it off."

"Magic as in a curse?" Matthias asked.

"Curse or gift? It's a matter of perspective," the old man said, shifting his hands like a scale.

Matthias shot him a skeptical look.

"How do you feel? Deep inside?" the man asked him.

"Sad," Matthias answered.

The mask began to squirm in Matthias's hands. Surprised, he dropped it, catching only a glimpse of the face it made before it hitting the stone. The amorphous material had shaped a face for itself. A sad face. It hit the stone and returned to its original state of facelessness.

The old man cackled as Matthias approached the mask with caution and picked it up again.

"What do you want people to see, even though you feel sad?" the old man asked.

"Happiness," Matthias answered and watched as a smile almost split the mask in two. "This is beautiful," he said in awe.

"Perfect for a performer like yourself," the old man stated.

Matthias looked to the young boy, who had been quiet for some time.

"The mask doesn't make the man, the man makes the mask," the child whispered.

"Go ahead!" the old man shouted. "Put it on!"

Matthias turned away so neither would see his face. He slipped off his mask, then put on the helmet. It felt as though he had plunged into a steadily moving river. There was no pain, just a gentle sensation that washed over his face, searching for all of his secrets. The exterior of the mask began to move, twisting and turning into hideous contortions. Testing each emotion until it finally rested in a subtle grin. Matthias turned back but both the old man and the child were gone.

Due to the nature of this mask, he never had to take it off; and he never did. A year passed, and Matthias still found no peace. Matthias continued performing in the theatre. In Anastasia's absence, he had become a renowned actor throughout the region and places beyond.

When a terrible plague struck Perditus, Matthias's father decided to take their troupe on the road. As the plague continued to spread, they traveled further to distant parts of the world. The troupe made a lot of money, and Matthias's fame continued to grow. He became the envy of all men, known and defined by the mask he had chosen. He attended parties and made many acquaintances; but no matter where he went, he always stopped by local shops, looking for quilts, or more accurately, a quilt seller. He often wondered what had become of Anastasia and what could have been. *What if I had just taken off my mask? What if I had let her in completely? What if I had stayed with her? Then maybe I could be the one kissing her.* One night he decided he wanted nothing more to do with masks, but when he tried to take his off, he could not.

A king, by the name of Solomon, heard of Matthias and his enchanted mask. Although he lived quite a distance away, the King requested that Matthias's troupe perform for his private party. Matthias's troupe packed up and traveled very far to perform for His Majesty. The night came and went. As always, Matthias left the audience wanting more. After the show, Solomon summoned Matthias to appear in front of all of his royal guests. Matthias entered the room, his mask blank. He sensed their intimidation from seeing him up close.

None of them wore masks. The King broke the heavy air the room held with a cordial greeting and his friendly nature.

"It is a pleasure to meet you, Matthias," he began. "You gave a most splendid performance tonight."

Matthias bowed. "It's a great honor to have performed for you. Your approval means very much to me, Your Majesty."

Solomon smiled. "I hear where you come from all men wear masks. My city must seem quite odd to you."

Matthias looked around the room. There were dozens of beautiful women and well-dressed men, all of their faces bare to the world, but not honest. He had seen this many times in his travels.

"I can assure you, my King, I am not the only one in this room wearing a mask," he answered.

"Well spoken," the King said, impressed. "Be that as it may, you have done a great service to me, traveling all this way and performing for us. I wish to repay you. If you desire a feast, you shall have it. Money? I can give you gold. The company of a woman? You shall have a wife. Ask me for anything short of my kingdom, and it shall be yours. What do you desire?"

Matthias let his head sink. "With all due respect, what I desire, no one can give me."

Everyone remained silent, unsure of how to react to this statement. The King shifted his weight, intrigued. "And what is it that you desire?"

"A young boy once told me, 'The mask doesn't make the man, the man makes the mask.' I did not understand what he meant at the time, but he tried to warn me. Our masks represent us, we must be careful which one or ones we choose to make our own. Some masks are easy to put on, and some can be very hard to take off. My King, although no one will understand it, my desire is to be free of my mask."

Everyone looked at Matthias with looks of disbelief

or disgust. They only understood the desire for riches, not for truth, except Solomon. Sympathy showed on his face.

"Leave us," he said to his guests.

Taken aback by the order, many guests left the party as well as the room, offended.

Once Solomon and Matthias were alone, the King reached into his robes and produced a piece of parchment.

"No one knows of this. I suggest you keep it that way." He handed the parchment to Matthias.

Mathias opened it and saw it was a map.

"Where does it lead?" he asked.

"There is a legend of a fountain whose waters can heal a man on his deathbed. I have kept it a secret so someday when I had need of it I could live forever. I do not know if the fountain is real or if it can help you, but if there is anything in the world that can help you, this is it."

Matthias looked at the map again, understanding what it meant. He folded it and tried to hand it back but Solomon refused.

"Do not tempt me," he said. "I have yet to meet a king who should live forever."

"I believe I may have," Matthias answered, as he put the map in his pocket.

Matthias left the palace that night, not telling anyone. He knew his friends and family would not understand, so he left without saying goodbye. He left everything behind and went off in search of a fountain, which he knew may or may not, exist. He left through the town, buying supplies along the way.

He followed the map for days, and it brought him away from the city, away from all life in general. The few people he met along the road did not ask the nature of his journey, and when the roads began to end Matthias found himself crossing a desert. He continued on, in spite of these things, even when his water supply ran dry, knowing if nothing changed he would die. The sun continued to rise high, and Matthias fell to his knees, exhausted. He felt the sand burn over his body as the wind rose and he fell to the ground. *I was a fool chasing this thing, not because I knew it was real, but simply because I wished it to be. I will die out here.* He looked up to see a small pond of water in front of him. He threw himself into the watering hole, drinking greedily. He restocked his water supply and, in spite of his desire to turn back, he forged ahead. Shortly after, he found a deserted ancient palace, and in the palace he found the fountain.

Although he could not see anyone, Matthias ascended the steps leading to the fountain with caution, assuming there would be a guardian of the mystical water. He watched as the water trickled out of spigots and into the body of the fountain. On the top rested a torch, burning over the water which seemed to emit a sweet fragrance.

Matthias stared at it for a moment, admiring the intricate artwork. Then he approached it and looked down at his reflection in the water. He saw his mask, and he saw a boy and an older gentleman. He quickly jumped back. The man stood next to where he had been, still looking down into the water, hiding his face. The boy, on the other hand, sat on the edge of the fountain facing Matthias.

"Why are you here?" the man asked, upset. "Is my mask not good enough?"

"I'm afraid it's too good. I have worn this mask for far too long. I wish to know who I am," Matthias answered defiantly.

"What if I give you another mask?" the older man pleaded. "It's too dangerous, Matthias, to see what's underneath! It could be anything!"

Matthias felt fear creep into his heart once more. *I could be anything...I could be nothing.* But he expelled the thoughts. *At least I will be genuine.* He looked to the young boy, who once again whispered under the overdramatic cries of the man. He spoke only two words.

"Matthias...come."

Matthias approached the fountain again. He turned to the old man who still whined.

"Depart from me," Matthias whispered.

The man stopped.

"What?" he asked in disbelief.

"Depart from me!" Matthias shouted.

The old man turned to face Matthias and cried out as he began to disappear. Matthias felt his stomach churn and his heart race. The man wore no mask. The man, screaming at him in outrage, had no face.

The man disappeared, and the screaming stopped abruptly. Matthias sank to the floor panting. *I could have ended up like him!* He turned to face the boy as though the boy could hear his thoughts. The little boy looked at him and smiled a warm smile and pointed to the fountain. Matthias then remembered his whole purpose for being there. He stood up and faced the waters. He saw the blank mask staring back at him. Then, in a moment of faith, he lowered his head and plunged it deep into the water. At first it felt like ice, then it burned like fire. He could feel the mask shifting over his skin. He reached into the fountain to take it off. His hand tugged and it felt as though he were tearing his face off. He screamed under the water as it began to let go of the flesh it had come to know so well. He peeled it off, leaving it in the fountain with the many others he had not noticed before. He pulled his head out of the fountain and felt the wondrous sensation of the water running down his skin. He looked to the boy, who smiled and said a single word.

"Look."

Matthias smoothed back his hair and looked into the fountain. There he saw himself, beautiful and genuine, and he found peace.

Matthias stood on the hill letting the wind whip his body. Winter had come, but this was his time and he would not let the weather disturb it. He had traveled to many nations and received much praise. He had crossed a desert and, after many years of hiding, confronted himself. He had returned to Perditus to find her. Now he knew who he really was. Now he had no need for masks. He wanted her to know he had removed the mask. He returned to her grandmother, and she had sent him here to the hill overlooking the city, the hill with the stone which read, "Here lies Anastasia, beloved wife, taken by the plague." And next to it laid another stone which read, "Here lies Jason, beloved husband, taken by the plague."

Matthias bowed his head in a moment of silence. *So this is the man who got to kiss your lips.* He knew they had been happy together, Anastasia's grandmother had told him as much. She had also told him that Anastasia's husband had always been truthful with her, surrendering his mask. Matthias had been happy to hear these things. He remembered the night Anastasia had left him. He could still see her face. He could still feel her hands as she kissed the cheek of his mask. He could still hear her voice saying, "Goodbye, Matthias." He let one tear roll down his cheek and land on the ground before her stone, letting it be his kiss goodbye.

"Goodbye, Anastasia," he whispered, and he left.

THE LEGEND OF POLARIS

2

"You're thinking about her," Christopher said, as he watched David stare into his mug of ale. After many years of friendship and being students together Christopher knew just about everything concerning David, and he read him like a book.

"Aren't you?" David answered, looking up with a smirk.

"Yes, but not in the same way," Christopher countered.

The two young men had arrived in the city of Loredana earlier that day, and, though they now sat unnoticed in the corner of an inn, they had drawn too much attention to themselves upon their entrance.

David's eyes returned to his ale. It was rare for David to run out of words. Christopher decided he would address the thing neither of them wanted to talk about yet knew must be discussed.

"You're going to see her, aren't you?" Christopher asked.

"When a princess has requested your presence, it would be impolite to make her wait, wouldn't it?" David asked.

"I think she's already forgotten you," Christopher said, with dry sarcasm.

"I think you're jealous. Why don't you come with me?" David asked, raising his mug to his lips before adding with a laugh, "You can keep me in line."

This time it was Christopher's turn to stare into his mug.

"No," he said. "I think it's best if at least one of us keeps a low profile," he finished with a wicked smile.

David laughed.

The two young men ordered another round of drinks before Christopher looked at David.

"One should not keep a princess waiting," he said.

David looked out a nearby window. It was dusk, and a soft mist had begun to fall, as it often did at night in Loredana.

"What about you?" David asked.

"I have eaten well, drunk even better, and we have already paid for a room here for ten days," Christopher answered. "I won't be sitting up worrying about you, if that's what you are asking."

David laughed before finishing his drink and rising.

"I'll try not to wake you when I return," he answered, dropping a few coins on the table.

He turned and headed to the door, looking back once to see Christopher wave at him in a patronizing fashion, before trying to flag down a waitress. David shook his head as he stepped into the mist and began to head in the direction of the castle.

Loredana was a smaller city, walled in by ramparts, and the castle could be seen from just about every direction. David felt grateful he would not have to ask anyone for directions. He liked the people and enjoyed their conversations but he and Christopher had had a full day. They had arrived in the mid-afternoon and, after finding an inn, had begun to wander and explore the city. He had been looking for Christopher in a crowd, when the people had parted before him as if they were waves and he stood on the bow of a ship. That was when he had seen her; Adrienne, the Princess of Loredana, trotting towards him on her horse. He had been so taken with her, he had not noticed the people behind him had also begun to split and back away. He stood oblivious in the center of the road, like an outlaw, or perhaps an idiot, coming to challenge the local authority. One of her royal guards had shoved him to the ground and raised his weapon to beat David when the Princess had commanded her man to step away. She had dismounted and, noticing David's robes, asked if he was from the Academy.

The "Academy" was what everyone called it. That is, when people spoke of the school deep within the mountain, Polaris. Most people thought it was a school for young wizards, as every student was given a plain gray robe to wear throughout their time there. David's parents had been farmers and had saved for many years to be able to send him to the Academy.

He had admitted he was a student of the Academy, knowing this simple admission could cost him his life. He had somehow sensed this was not her intention. Instead she had instructed her guards to leave him and, as the captain of the guard had helped her onto her horse, she had looked back at him and requested his presence at the castle at his earliest convenience.

He raised his hood as the rain began to fall heavier. He slowed his pace in hopes that by the time he arrived at the castle, the Princess would be asleep and he could leave a message. He still had qualms about his visit, not for fear of death but rather for something he could not discern. He felt as if he were walking into a dark, empty cave. There was nothing to fear, and yet there was some ominous feeling he could not shake.

His internal struggle grew with each step, and he debated returning to the inn and forgetting the whole escapade; but he could not. He wanted to see her again. He wanted to look into the depths of her eyes, and listen to the stories they would tell. He imagined being in her presence.

As David approached the castle gate, two guards came out to question him, before a third recognized him by his robes. He then waited with the guards as they sent word to the Princess. After some time, he was escorted by two new guards into the castle. Walking through the tight, quiet corridors of stone vaguely reminded him of the Academy. It was not a long journey, just long enough for David's anxiety to begin to dissipate. Then they passed through the threshold of the throne room. He wasn't sure if the rainwater had made his hands wet or if it was the clammy sweat that comes before speaking to a room full of people. He guessed it was the latter as his heart began to drum a furious rhythm.

The throne room was large and circular with marble tiered platforms that rose up in the center to hold a throne. There sat the Princess. David respectfully bowed and waited to be addressed.

"David!" she cried, "I knew you were coming. I just knew it!"

She laughed, amused by David's clear confusion from her casual greeting, and gestured for him to come toward her. He obeyed. She rose from the throne and descended the steps towards him as she spoke.

"I am Princess Adrienne. My father is the King, and he's presently away at war. There's no need for all of the formalities with me."

David stared at her, confused. "I am afraid I don't understand, Princess."

"Please, call me Adrienne."

"Adrienne," he corrected himself. "You wished to speak with me."

It was not a statement but a question.

"I have always desired to meet a wizard," she said, blushing.

"I do not wish to disappoint you, but I am not a wizard," he corrected.

"But you wear the robes of the Academy?" she countered, in a diplomatic tone.

"I am afraid many people believe the Academy teaches young wizards, due to our attire and our concealment from the world." David began carefully, for fear of offending the Princess. "But the Academy does no such thing. It is simply a school; specifically for doctors, lawyers, and philosophers."

"Oh," she said, contemplating his words.

David stood in silence, watching her. She was so elegant, so regal, and yet so young.

"And which do you study?" she asked.

"I am a student of philosophy."

David watched her face illuminate.

"What can you tell me about 'students of philosophy'? Or can you not tell me because it's a secret?" she asked.

David smiled a reassuring smile. "I can tell you anything. What would you like to know?"

"Why are you here in Loredana?" she asked.

"Honestly, I don't know," he said.

She stared at him, puzzled.

"The final step before graduating the Academy is to take a trip to practice your craft. Doctors go to towns and cities to heal people. Lawyers leave to practice the law. And philosophers," he paused. "I confess I don't know what it is we are supposed to do."

"What is it exactly that a philosopher does?" the Princess asked.

"We search for and study the truth," David answered.

"Then you must be here to learn," she stated.

"Learn what?" he pressed.

"About my people and what truth is to them."

David considered this.

"I think I'd like to learn this philosophy," Adrienne announced. "Would you teach me?"

"It would be an honor," David answered.

"And I can teach you magic," Adrienne said, with excitement. She watched as David's face changed to a look of disapproval. "I'm sorry I didn't tell you. You must hate me," she said, her face crestfallen.

"I don't hate anyone," David assured her. "I knew you were a magician."

"How?" she whispered.

"I don't know...I just knew."

"Then why did you come? I hear the students of the Academy hate magicians."

"We don't hate them. We just fundamentally disagree with them. Philosophers search for the truth, magicians look for ways to mask and distort it," David paused to see if he should continue. "I hear the Master Magician was a philosopher until he was expelled from the school."

"He wasn't expelled. He left! And he was right to leave! They would not permit the use of any magic!" she stated with a hint of defiance in her tone.

"Because it's dangerous," retorted David.

"It is not! Have you ever tried it?" Adrienne countered.

"No," David admitted.

"Not even white magic?" she continued.

"It is forbidden. Philosophers don't use any kind of magic, ever," David explained.

"Well, we will have to fix that. Here, let me teach you," she said, reaching into her pocket and producing a small orb-like object.

"Please don't," he said, covering her hands with his, masking and avoiding what she held. Her eyes locked with his, and he realized she could have him executed for touching her. He became conscious of her touch. Her hands felt smooth and delicate, the hands of a princess.

"Alright," she whispered, her eyes catching his.

"Tell me about how you became a magician," David said, releasing his grasp.

Adrienne blushed. "I never planned on becoming a magician. After my mother's death my father became obsessed with war. He is constantly away, either ending battles or starting new ones. Sometimes it feels like he's not out to get his enemies but rather he wants to kill himself."

"Losing a loved one is a very difficult thing. We all grieve in different ways," David offered.

"It's no excuse to treat your daughter as if she died too." Adrienne answered, her temper flaring for a moment.

David nodded in silence.

"It was the plague," she said, a tear slipping from her eye. "The only thing my father couldn't protect her from."

David wanted to offer comfort but feared words would fall short, and a friendly touch would be inappropriate.

She looked away, regaining her quiet composure.

"I have grown up alone in this place," she continued. "At first it was a childish desire to play tricks on people for amusement. It was all fun and harmless really.

"When I heard the Master Magician had come to town, I went to him, and after being amazed by his tricks, I begged him to take me as an apprentice. It has been years now, and I have learned a great deal from him. Oh, David, you must let me introduce the two of you, when he returns to visit!"

The words hit David like arrows. She knew the Master Magician, and he was her tutor.

"I don't know," he said.

"Perhaps you're right," she said, stifling a yawn. "It's too soon."

"It's getting late, Princess. You should rest," David suggested.

"I don't want to," she sighed, "but you're probably right."

Taking him by the elbow, she accompanied him to the

door. As she opened it a guard appeared, awaiting instruction. The Princess commanded him to deliver David to his lodging. Then she turned to David.

"You will come back, won't you?" she asked.

"Of course," he said with a smile.

The Princess quickly kissed him on the cheek and left him standing speechless, his face filling with heat. Then she disappeared, and the guard led him by the shoulder out of the castle. He contemplated his visit the whole journey back to the inn. He recalled every word she had spoken, wondering if they possessed some hidden meaning. He couldn't subdue his smile. Although probably intended to be a friendly gesture, he could not help but wonder if perhaps there was more behind the kiss.

David awoke to the sound of a rooster crowing. At the Academy the students had awoken each morning to the gentle toll of a bell. David rose from his bottom bunk and went to the window of the room. He opened the wooden shutters and saw the rooster down below look up at him with a quizzical cock of its head, as if wondering what had taken him so long to respond to its call. It crowed again. The sun had barely begun to rise and David decided he hated roosters.

He walked to the basin of water which had been left out and washed his face and, after seeing Christopher was not in the top bunk, headed down to the main part of the tavern for breakfast. Christopher was already at a table eating. David got his food from the innkeeper's wife, who was cooking eggs over the fire, before joining Christopher at the table.

"How long have you been awake?" David asked.

"Awhile," Christopher answered, in his usual cryptic way. "I was not out late on secret errands," he teased.

"Nor was I," David answered. "There is no secret. You

know where I was."

Even over the din of breakfast the rooster's crow could be heard. David winced.

"I'm going to kill that wretched animal," he said.

Christopher laughed.

"So," David continued, "Do you have any idea what we are doing here?"

Christopher chewed his eggs thoughtfully before answering. "Well, we have ten days before we must return to the Academy. The other students will be practicing their crafts, healing people or practicing law, in the other cities… and we," he paused. "I think we are just here to help people."

"Interesting," David said. "Adrienne suggested we are here to learn."

"I would imagine it's a bit of both," he stated. "One should learn from all situations."

David took another bite of food before Christopher pressed, "So are you going to leave me in suspense, or are you going to tell me about your visit?"

David looked at the table and smiled, memories of the prior night flooding his mind. For a moment he forgot they were in the middle of a tavern in a foreign city, and it felt as if they were back at the Academy, Christopher teasing him about some crush in front of their friends.

"I'm tempted to leave you in suspense," David answered.

Christopher laughed, knowing part of David's ability to deal with life was to talk about it. He would sooner learn to fly than he would to keep his mouth shut.

"She's lonely," David stated. "She's a princess with an absent father. She has maids and servants but no friends. No real conversations or connections."

Christopher studied David as he gave his synopsis.

"Except maybe," David paused, "for the Master Magician."

He had expected a look of surprise or even an outburst

from Christopher, neither of which came. Christopher listened, hands folded on the table. After a moment of silence he chimed in.

"Are you surprised to learn she is a magician?" he asked.

David shrugged. "I was just surprised to find she knew the Master Magician."

Christopher didn't comment.

"She wants to learn philosophy," David continued.

"I had a feeling she might," Christopher answered. "So you will be returning to her?"

"Yes." David answered. "Do you think it unwise?"

Christopher pondered the question for a moment before answering. "Not at this time."

After breakfast, Christopher and David left their lodging to explore the city of Loredana.

Anxiety built up in David as they walked through the city market. The Academy had been small, and he had never seen so many people in one place. Vendors lined the congested streets, waving and shouting, trying to capture some passerby's attention. After having to speak with two separate merchants, trying to leave each without losing any of his money, David was quick to learn not to look anyone directly in the eyes. Occasionally a child would brush by David's leg, unaccompanied as he or she ran through the crowd. The sounds of customers arguing with merchants and husbands with wives filled David's ears and somewhere in the distance he could hear a baby crying. Everyone appeared to be in a great hurry, giving birth to a mild form of chaos as people pushed their way through the crowd. In the midst of it all, David could not help but feel a little lost.

By midmorning, David and Christopher had explored several sections of the city and had developed a plan. They only had enough money to pay for their food and lodging during their ten day visit to Loredana. They made their way out to the countryside and found a farmer who was willing to spare a few coins for a bit of work. He was an older gentleman, a widower. He had told them running a farm was hard work, even more so when you did it alone. The two spent several hours in the fields harvesting wheat alongside him. After the sun had reached its zenith they collected their few coins and told him they would return the next day if he would like. He accepted their offer.

By late-afternoon, David and Christopher had once more found themselves in the strange cacophony of the city. They used the few coins they had gained from their work to purchase several loaves of bread and a cheap but sturdy sack to carry it all in. Then they began to roam the poorer sections of the city. Tearing the bread into smaller portions, they distributed it to whomever they could. Even after they had exhausted their supply of bread, they remained, caring for the sick and speaking with them, learning their stories and their ways.

By dusk they returned to their lodging, tired and very hungry themselves. They each ordered a mug of ale and received a generous portion of the stew that had been prepared earlier in the day. They found a table to sit at and were both relieved to be off of their feet. Over dinner they discussed the events of the day and the people they had met: the widowed farmer and his difficult work, the baker who would charge you less if you knew a bit of local gossip, and the girl with the disingenuous smile sewn on her face they had met in the darker section of the city.

Once they had finished their supper, they ordered another round of drinks. They sat in silence, enjoying the revelry of their neighboring tables, watching the other men and women who had also experienced a full day's work.

"You're going to see her, aren't you?" Christopher asked, the question coming from nowhere.

"Yes." David answered, a strange sense of guilt covering him. There was nothing wrong with his decision; in fact, it was a good opportunity. The Princess had asked him to visit her to discuss philosophy. How would it appear if he did not show up? It may have been somewhere inside of himself he felt it was not a wise decision, or perhaps he simply did not want to leave Christopher's good company.

"I know," Christopher responded.

David detected concern in his friend's voice, which he almost questioned. Instead he nodded and rose from the table.

"Be careful," Christopher warned.

"Always," David replied, his typical response.

David arrived at the castle and was surprised to find Adrienne had left a personal guard to wait for him. The same guard who had recognized him the day before greeted David and introduced him to his personal escort, another guard who stood close behind. The man did not offer a greeting outside of a simple nod and then beckoned for David to follow.

He led David through several hallways and corridors and David admired the tapestries and other artwork that decorated the palace. It wasn't until they passed the empty throne room that David began to question their journey. He asked where they were going, but the guard continued walking. David froze. If he turned back now he was pretty sure he could still remember most of the way back to the entrance. His guard stopped with him, and, after giving David a moment, he gestured for him to follow again and continued walking. Together they ascended a staircase and came to a gold-plated door. The guard knocked twice and stepped back, standing at attention.

"Enter," someone called.

The guard opened the door and motioned for David to enter.

As David stepped through the door, he felt as if he had stepped into another world. Up until this point the castle had been just a castle. A stone castle surrounded by a walled city and a bridge, which drew the line between the common folk and the King's home. This room, however, looked as if it were from some distant land. Warm candlelight and the pale rays of the moon provided a low illumination. Exotic flowers surrounded the edges of the beautifully designed marble floor, which had been crafted with raised and lowered sections. The lower sections seemed to be for entertaining guests, David assumed, as he noted the cushions in each. The raised section, however, flowed like a frozen river, which in turn led to the center of the room where a large bed lay. Several pearl-white marble pillars held up the ceiling and, on the far side of the room, David could see a moonlit balcony, which was separated from the main room by translucent drapes.

The sound of a light rain met his ears along with the sweet sing-song voice of the Princess, who rose from the edge of her bed and crossed the room towards him.

"You came back," she said.

"Did you ever doubt me?" he asked, not meaning to sound quite as teasing as he did.

"No, not you." She smiled, embracing him.

"It's late. I hope you don't mind meeting here," she said, motioning around her room.

"Not at all," he said.

"Where do we begin?" she asked.

"With the Fathers of Philosophy," he replied.

"This sounds more like a history lesson," she said, stepping down into one of the lower portions of her room and sitting on a cushion.

"Truth is not limited by time," he answered, sitting close but across from her.

"Then let's start with the here and now," she mused.

"Why bother with men who died thousands of years ago?"

"It's not that simple." David replied. "At the creation of the world there was chaos and strife. The Ancients themselves came down to teach the Fathers the truths of life, which became philosophy. It is one of the few times in history the Ancients have ever walked among men."

"And who are the Ancients?" Adrienne asked.

"No one knows. Maybe gods? Angels, perhaps? Some individuals claimed to have seen them in times of extreme peril, but, historically speaking, the teaching of the fathers is the only instance in which multiple people saw them."

"Interesting," Adrienne sighed. She still did not seem impressed. If anything she seemed bored, looking down at her fingernails.

Perhaps this is not the best approach, David thought before asking, "Why don't you tell me what you believe?"

Adrienne looked up, smiling.

"I believe we are here and now. I believe we live to experience, and I believe if it's not hurting anyone it's fine," she said, leaning in close to him as she said each word.

David realized the room was rather dim. A brief wind passed through, rustling the thin drapes and tugging at the small flames of each candle. A sweet but subtle fragrance filled his nostrils, and the tiny lights reflected from her eyes. The room around him began to fade away into the dimness, and he saw only her face looking back at him, studying him, searching him. David debated what to say, once again afraid of offending her.

"So you don't believe in things beyond the here and now?"

"If there are then it's as you say... beyond." She smiled, leaning back on her cushion. "Let people be people. We live, we die. It's as simple as that."

"Then what is the point?" he asked.

44

"Whatever matters to you," she answered, glancing at her fingernails again.

"What if I believe in destruction?" he pressed.

"As I said, if it's not hurting anyone, it's fine," she looked up, searching his eyes again. "Besides, no one in their right mind wants destruction."

David didn't respond. This conversation was not going as he had intended. He almost laughed at himself. What had he expected? To win over a princess in a brief conversation? He watched her as she looked up from her fingers. She was so full of life and so beautiful. Dark locks framed her face like a precious pearl.

"What?" she asked.

"Nothing," David said, shaking his head as if to wake himself from a daze. "What is the first thing you were taught in magic?"

"A flare."

"A flare?"

"May I?" she asked, in a patronizing tone.

David nodded.

She rose and crossed the room to a desk. She returned and produced a coin, holding out both hands, one with the coin resting flat against her palm and the other empty.

"A flare," she began, "is the way a magician controls his audience and guides them."

As she said this there was a quick flash of light on the empty hand. David glanced at the flash and in the millisecond it took the coin disappeared from her other hand.

"It's simple misdirection," he stated, impressed by the flare but not by the trick.

"Not always," she said, extending her newly empty hand towards him. This time there was a quick flash and the coin appeared in the same hand. David stared at it in awe.

"It's juvenile, really," she said. "I think flares were

designed to give young magicians more confidence. Because if you are really good..." she twisted her wrist once over, then back, and the coin was gone. "You don't need it," she whispered.

David's mind began racing. Reason dictated this had merely been a trick, but his eyes would not agree. No matter how hard he reasoned he could not figure out how she had done it.

"Well," he said, clearing his throat, "the Fathers of Philosophy are like flares. They show us where to look."

It didn't sound as clever as he had hoped when he heard it out loud. He could tell by her face she was waiting for him to ask how she had done it. He refrained. His purpose there was to discuss philosophy, not magic. He watched the candlelight dance in her eyes. They each waited for the other to break the silence, but it was a comfortable silence. They sat simply gazing at each other, locked in a childish game of trying to read the other's thoughts.

"You should stay here," she said, breaking the spell.

"I'm sorry?" he asked, pulled from his thoughts.

"You should stay with me," she repeated. "Here in the castle. There are plenty of rooms, and it is clear we will not resolve philosophy in a night. We will need several nights at least."

"I'm afraid I must return to my companion," David answered.

"That's fine." She smiled, rising and motioning for him to do the same. "Think about it," she said, kissing him on the cheek again. She then turned David by the shoulders to face the guard who had led him to her chambers. He wondered how long the guard had been there, or if he had ever left.

"Interesting," Christopher said, once David finished

46

his retelling of the prior night's events, leaving out the part where the Princess had invited him to stay. He had arrived back at the tavern to find Christopher already asleep. David had reflected on the night's events over a single drink before lying in his own bed and falling asleep. In the morning, the two had eaten breakfast together and discussed their plans for the day. David had told his tale as they had begun to work once more for the old widowed farmer, cutting wheat.

"Maybe you shouldn't go back," Christopher suggested.

"Why is that?" David asked, swinging his scythe.

"The Princess doesn't seem to care for philosophy," Christopher said.

David's irritation began to grow inside of him.

"All good things take time, my friend," David said, defending her. "Like this wheat. It takes a full season for it to grow. It requires time and sacrifice."

"I know," Christopher answered, stopping to wipe the sweat from his brow. "But I think this will lead to time and compromise. Do you remember the difference?"

The heat of the afternoon sun was beating down upon them, and yet David felt a separate heat rise within him.

"Yes, Master Christopher," he answered, insulted. "To sacrifice is to give up something you want out of love. Compromise is surrendering something you believe to get the bare minimum."

"Don't patronize me. I'm trying to help," Christopher replied.

"Then help me," David grumbled, before collecting himself. "How do I teach her?"

Christopher stopped altogether and thought about this. "I can see you care about her," he began, "but this is not an exam. You can't just write down the answer and expect it to be over. We teach people the truth by how we live and what we leave behind."

David continued harvesting the wheat, listening but not acknowledging any of what his friend said. The anger within him had peaked. He had known Christopher would say these words. Not just because he knew Christopher so well, but because if their positions had been reversed, David would have said the same thing.

"It is true we have to meet people where they are at," Christopher continued. "It just feels like she is inviting you to join her. Does that make sense?" he asked.

David tensed at the phrase as she *had* invited him to join her, not in her beliefs per se, but in her castle.

"Was there anything else?" Christopher asked.

"No," David lied.

His first compromise.

The night rain had just begun to fall as David entered the marketplace. Most of the vendors and merchants had already packed their carts, but a few remained in hope of one final sale. David stopped at a small fruit stand and, after examining the apples, purchased one, leaving the man a little more money than necessary. He did this for two reasons. First, he figured if the merchant was here at this hour he must have someone depending on him, and David wanted to help. Second, he had used the transaction as an excuse to look around and see if he was being followed.

Christopher was no idiot. He knew David had continued to see Adrienne since their conversation in the field only a few days before. But David was afraid of the judgment which would come if he confessed to Christopher where he was going. They had needed a lie, or rather an excuse to ignore the truth, to spare them further confrontation. An excuse for him to leave each night. He had told Christopher that he would be out visiting the nearby churches and temples. He had said he wished to talk to the city's priests and learn more about their religious beliefs. Christopher had not questioned this. David felt ashamed but could not discern why. He had gone to see the Princess. He was trying to teach her. Wasn't that the point of this whole endeavor, to teach people?

David polished the apple on his robe as he continued on towards the castle in the rain, thunder gently rumbling in the distance.

Yes, he had seen a little magic; but he had only let Adrienne perform magic for him to show he cared about what mattered to her. He was fostering a connection and, in time, perhaps he could change her mind. It would be a delicate task, requiring time and sacrifice. David winced, remembering his conversation in the field with Christopher. The reality was that he was trying to do the right thing, and he wasn't hurting anyone. In fact, her magic tricks had seemed quite innocent and fun.

He continued on in his thoughts, still feeling the qualms he always did as he stepped onto the drawbridge and approached the castle gate. He had taken his first bite of the apple when he heard his name. He turned to see Christopher, looking disappointed.

"You've been following me," David accused.

"You've been lying," Christopher responded.

The rain seemed to fall heavier with his words.

"I'm here to help her," David said, his voice rising with a roll of thunder.

"You're here because you are infatuated," Christopher replied.

"What if I can save her!" David shouted.

"And what if she destroys you!" roared Christopher. "She's changed you."

Lightning shattered the sky, followed by a thunder crash, which seemed to shake the ground. Anger surged in

David. There would be no more arguing. This had become a crossroad, and he could no longer stand in the middle. He had to choose. He could return with Christopher, or he could stay and try to teach Adrienne. Why couldn't Christopher understand? They were here to help people, and he was helping Adrienne. He would teach her philosophy and be her friend, as she did not seem to have any. Both Christopher and Adrienne were David's friends, and he did not want to choose between them. Christopher's words rang in his ears with the thunder. *What if she destroys you? What if...?*

"We study the truth but that doesn't make us fortune tellers," David said. Then he turned towards the castle and entered the gate.

David stood, cold and wet from the rain, waiting for admission to see Adrienne. Although he had become familiar to the guards, there were still certain precautions and formalities to be observed. Listening to the soft sound of each drop of water dripping from his cloak, David felt like a man in a trance, hypnotized by the words of someone who had once been his closest friend. *What if she destroys you...?* He hadn't meant for it to happen, but one of his greatest childhood fears had become a reality. He had lost his best friend, his brother, and now stood alone. David closed his eyes, taking a deep breath, followed by a deeper sigh. He needed a clear mind. He needed a warm bed and sleep. He would deal with it tomorrow.

A small but warm tingling of excitement rose in his chest when the guard returned and motioned for him to follow. He would get to see Adrienne. Following close behind his escort, David entered the throne room.

When Adrienne saw him, she left her father's throne, gliding down the steps to embrace him. She stopped short when she saw his condition and wasted no time ordering one of the maids to see he had a warm bath and a fresh robe.

The bath rejuvenated his spirits, and the robe made him feel like a king. He was then escorted to a bedroom where he waited until the Princess came calling.

"Have you come to stay?" she asked hopefully, as he opened the door to greet her.

"If you wish, I shall," he answered.

"Well, I wish," she giggled. Then, sensing his discomfort, she inquired, "David, what's wrong?"

"It's nothing," he sighed. "I just had a fight with Christopher, and I'm afraid it has ended a very good friendship."

"I'm sorry. Was he the other student you traveled with?"

David nodded.

"And you were fighting about me?" she asked, an innocent look in her eyes.

David nodded again.

"I'm sorry," she whispered.

"It's not your fault," David reassured her with a weak smile.

"Here, let me cheer you up," said Adrienne, taking him by the hand and drawing him deeper into the room.

They sat on the edge of his bed and Adrienne reached over, taking both of his hands in hers, and turned his palms up. She flashed her girlish smile at him before staring with great intensity at his hands. She traced over parts of his palms with her thumbs.

"I see here you've had a sheltered life, spending little time in the world and much of your time in contemplation," she said, pointing to two intersecting lines. "This mark shows sorrow, pain, and anger. No doubt from your broken friendship." She paused for a moment and looked back at his eyes. "But that's not all, is it? There's a void of unspeakable depth. Much deeper than anything you believe can fill-"

"Deception will not cheer me, but thank you." David

began to retract his hands.

Adrienne looked embarrassed before regaining her charm. "You didn't let me finish," she whispered.

"I'm listening," he retorted.

Without missing a beat, she looked at him with her deep green eyes, locking him in her gaze. "I see you will be satisfied. Not now, but soon. Soon you will forget, and you will be pleased."

Their gaze held for a moment longer before she broke it off.

"It's late. I must go," she whispered. David walked her over to the door. Just before she left, she turned to face him one last time, as though she were waiting for him. He felt the sudden urge to kiss her and, for a moment, thought she might fulfill this desire. Then she departed without a word, leaving David confused and desperate to see her again.

The next morning David awoke in his new room. He pushed himself up from under the covers, resting his head against the headboard and his back on one of the many pillows. The spacious room had been well furnished with chairs, a table, the enormous bed, and even decorative paintings. David's room at the Academy had been nothing like this. For many years, he had lived in a small rectangular room that had resembled a prison cell more than a bedchamber. He had never minded it. It had been simple and served its purpose. Now here, lying in the bed, he decided it would not take him long to adjust to the change.

He rose to find a new set of clothes had been laid out for him. He looked to where he had left his Academy-issued robe the night before only to find it had been removed. He sat on the edge of the bed, his head in his hands, the events of the past few days catching up with him.

Christopher would return to the Academy in just a

few short days and David wondered what story would be told. Christopher would probably tell everybody how David had been a fool. How he had not wished to help people so much as he had wished to woo a beautiful princess. His mind reeled as he thought of everyone he had known at the Academy, imagining their shock and horror as they realized David had lied, left, and would not return. He would return though, wouldn't he? After he had taught the Princess philosophy. But David knew that most students who didn't return when they were supposed to, rarely ever returned at all.

He felt the fabric of his new clothes as he began to dress himself. Afraid to listen for his heart's answer, he rose and walked to the window, which overlooked the city. *No*, he thought. He and Christopher had been best friends. Christopher would not slander him. He would tell them all the truth. He ran his fingers through his hair. *What is the truth?* he wondered.

He heard Adrienne's soft footsteps approaching on the stone and waited for her to address him. Just the sound of her sweet voice could make him smile, but, as he turned to her, he could tell something was wrong.

"Adrienne, what's wrong?" he asked, concerned.

"David, I don't know how to ask you this, but I really want to introduce you to the Master Magician. I know you just lost a good friend, and I think it would help to take your mind off of things. It would mean a lot to me."

David shook his head. "I'm not allowed to participate in this kind of lie. It's too dangerous. I really shouldn't have even let you show me what you did."

"But why can't you learn magic?" Adrienne whined. "It's not dangerous like your teachers said. It's just a bunch of fun, harmless tricks. I promise! Don't you trust me?"

"I do trust you. I just…I don't know," replied David, unconvinced about the whole thing.

Adrienne snuggled in close to his arm. "Tell you what, I will start to teach, and as soon as you think it's too much, we can stop."

David hesitated, considering her offer. "All right, sounds reasonable."

Adrienne's deep green eyes brightened. "You're going to love it!" she exclaimed. "I must prepare. Go to the gardens after lunch, and I will meet you there."

Without another word she turned and left him alone with his thoughts.

A servant brought his lunch to his room. Though the whole experience was something quite foreign to him, he found it refreshing. At the Academy all students ate together; though it was good to see friends, sometimes it felt better to be alone with one's thoughts. This was one of those times. A lot had changed in a short time, and David wanted to think without interruption. He was also certain if he began wandering around the castle, it would have led to many conversations with the guards.

After finishing his meal, David left his room, finding his escort waiting for him. He asked where he could find the gardens, explaining his situation. Just as before, the escort simply nodded and began to lead David through the castle

David still felt uneasy about Adrienne's request. She was going to teach him about magic. He didn't even want to imagine what Christopher would say, but she had made a solid point. *If there's no true power behind magic, then there is nothing to be afraid of.*

They entered the gardens where Adrienne was waiting for him. She wore a light purple dress which hugged her figure. Groups of purple lilacs and white lilies complemented her. Their aroma seemed to emanate from her like a perfume.

David wondered if he had somehow stepped out of the castle and into a painting. He walked towards her over a small decorative bridge which had been installed over an artificial pond. He glanced down for a moment at the still waters, watching the fish. As his eyes returned to Adrienne he could not tell what was more breathtaking: the glory of the gardens he walked through or the woman standing within them.

She took him by both hands and stepped backwards through the branches of a willow into the shade. He watched as they swayed back into place, creating a sort of protective veil, a bubble for their own little world by the tree. She motioned for him to sit on the ground across from her.

"This is beautiful," he said. "For a moment I forgot I was in a castle."

"Which is why I had my father build it," she said, looking up at the tree. "For when I wanted to escape."

"Here," she said, handing him a small dagger.

David examined it, beautifully crafted, yet light, to his surprise. The handle had an artistic image of a snake entwined around it. It looked as though the blade was protruding from the serpent's mouth. David pricked his finger with the very tip of the blade and felt a drop of warm blood begin to run down his hand.

"Stab me," Adrienne commanded, a look of mischief on her face.

David looked at her in disbelief.

"N-No," he stammered. "I don't want to hurt you."

"You won't. You can't," replied Adrienne, grabbing David's hand and forcing the blade into her stomach. He watched her eyes bulge, and they seemed to cry out to him in agony and grief. The blade slid out of her as she fell back onto the ground. Lilacs petals surrounded her as if they had been left there by design, perfectly arranged to adorn her corpse. David stared, speechless, as the dagger slipped from his hand. She was so still. David inhaled sharply, about to scream for help, when Adrienne's eyes fluttered open.

"Did I scare you?" she asked.

David expelled the breath he had been holding in.

"But I... You..." He looked at the knife and back at her.

"Magic," she whispered, with a look which was clearly rehearsed. Still feeling his heart racing, David couldn't decide if he should be angry or give in to his curiosity. Adrienne made the choice for him. She picked up the dagger and, skillfully holding the flat of the blade, pushed it back inside its handle.

"But how did it not cut you?"

Adrienne pressed David's hand to her abdomen. He felt a small metal plate beneath her dress. David nodded as it all came together in his head.

"See? Fun and harmless," Adrienne laughed.

"I'm not sure if fun is the first word I would pick," David said, still trying to appear upset. Adrienne offered a playful smile.

"You're just angry because I tricked you," she said.

"Perhaps," he admitted. "Is that it?" he asked. "You have one trick designed to scare the life out of people?"

A smile formed on Adrienne's lips along with the beginnings of a retort but no words were spoken. David noted a vibrancy in her eyes he didn't think had been there a moment ago. An idea had just come to her.

"I know that look," he said. "What are you thinking?"

"Do you trust me?" she asked.

"Yes," he answered.

Adrienne rose and stepped behind the tree's trunk. When she reemerged she had two common cloaks in her hand. She handed one to David.

"Put this on and follow me," she said. "Pull your hood up. We don't want to get caught."

Adrienne led David away from the willow and to the garden wall. She began to remove some of the rocks, revealing a hole just big enough for the two of them to squeeze through one at a time. Two thoughts crossed David's mind. First, she had done this before, and second, she had planned this from the start. They replaced the rocks, and she led him away from the castle and out into the city, passing through many of the beautiful sections and into the darker ones.

She slowed her pace as they approached an old, dingy tavern with a sign over the door that read, *Red Raven Tavern.* Several fat, old drunks sat on the front steps, making comments at Adrienne. She didn't seem to mind. *This is no place for a princess,* David thought, and debated asking her if she wanted to leave.

One of the drunks stood and began coming towards them. David stepped in front of Adrienne, not sure what he intended to do. He had never been in a fight before, and the Academy certainly hadn't trained him for this.

"You gonna be the big man?" the drunk man said, close enough now David could feel his breath. "Wanna impress your girly?"

Before David could answer, there was a quick flash of light. The drunk man pushed David out of the way, and David stumbled, his hands turning to fists as he regained his balance. He turned to find the drunk on his knees before Adrienne.

"Please, Eris!" the man howled. "I didn't know it was you! I swear I didn't know!"

He was down far enough to kiss her feet. Adrienne removed her hood with an air of drama.

"My friend, there is nothing to forgive," she said with a laugh. The tension left the air.

As if the world had shifted from a tragedy into a comedy play, David watched as the other drunks stood up.

"You dumb nincompoop!" one of them yelled. "It's Eris!"

Another ran down and kicked the man on the ground out of the way, ushering Adrienne towards the door of the tavern.

"Begging your pardon, Miss Eris!" he said, flustered. "We didn't mean none of what we said. We was just kiddin' around is all!" He turned to David. "I sees you brought a friend!" he exclaimed, shaking David's hand a little too fast and a little too long before motioning for both of them to follow him. He continued on with apologies and told Adrienne how excited everyone was going to be, all the while referring to her as "Eris."

When they got to the door, the drunk man flung it open with all the hoopla he could muster and shouted out over the noise of the bar that "Eris, the Magic Girl" had returned.

As they entered the tavern, everybody stood and cheered. Someone handed Adrienne a fresh drink from the bar. They shuffled her up onto a tiny, rather pathetic stage, and the cheering got even louder. "Eris, the Magic Girl" had made quite a name for herself. David found himself a seat in the corner and watched as she raised her hands. Silence followed, and, as if spellbound, all eyes turned from the bar to her.

Eris was more loved than any princess. David watched her performance, admiring the simple yet elegant design each of her deceptions held. Most tricks involved sleight-of-hand, while others had props like the fake dagger. She enamored the crowd with her performance, and the more David watched, the more he wanted to learn.

After the better portion of an hour, she announced she would be performing her final trick, motioning for David to join her on the stage.

"This is my assistant," she started. "What's your name?" she whispered to David.

"David," he replied, a bit confused by the question.

"This is a show, a performance, give it some spice!" she hissed, becoming aggravated. "This is my assistant!" she shouted again to the crowd.

"Ulysses, Master of Trickery," he responded, with

audacity. The crowd cheered. Adrienne shot him a look that told him he could do better but was on the right track. Careful to avoid the audience's gaze, she handed him the serpent dagger. "There will be blood this time, but don't be afraid," she whispered. "Give them a show."

David had always hated trial by fire. Whenever he learned something new, he wished he could practice it in secret until he had perfected it, but this was not an option. He had no time to prepare. He had to perform. The crowd fell silent, and all eyes were on him. He became uncomfortable as slight tremors coursed through his hands. His mouth became dry and he feared he might choke as he addressed the crowd for the first time.

"Once upon a time..." He stopped and looked to Adrienne, who gave an encouraging smile. "There was a beautiful princess." He gestured to Adrienne and the crowd roared. A small smirk began to crawl across his face as his idea came to life. "And there was a young traveler who fell in love with her." David shrugged his shoulders, indicating himself. The crowd hooted as Adrienne blushed. "But her stepfather," David continued, pulling his hood up over his head and dropping his voice, "her stepfather was an evil man and did not want a rightful heir to the kingdom. Thus, he had the Princess killed." David brandished the dagger and, with the speed of a snake, plunged it into Adrienne's stomach. The crowd went silent. Adrienne's face contorted into stages of pain and sorrow. David retracted the knife, his hands red and sticky. He watched as blood began to gush from her wound, soaking a dark crimson stain into her light purple dress. The crowd gasped. Adrienne's eyes fluttered and David caught her gracefully as she collapsed into his arms. All eyes were on the young woman in sheer disbelief and horror.

"What have you done!" yelled a man from the crowd. Others joined him, crying out in rage. As though they had been hypnotized, David silenced them with a wave of his hand.

"The story is not finished…" David removed his hood and paused.

"There was an Ancient wandering the earth," he continued, "who heard the cry of the young traveler, when he found his lover dead, and seeing the purity of their love he intervened. As you all know, the Ancients are not mere men, and they can take different forms. This Ancient came to the traveler as a small breeze, whispering one of the oldest truths there is." David paused, putting a hand to his ear for effect.

"True love may conquer anything… even death itself," he whispered, just loud enough for the audience to hear.

David sank to his knees and, cradling her body in his arms, kissed Adrienne's lips. He laid her body back on the floor with care and waited. Her eyes shot open, as she took a deep, over-emphasized breath so the crowd could see. Everybody cheered as David helped Adrienne to her feet and embraced her.

"How was that for showmanship?" David asked, speaking low so only Adrienne would hear as the crowd roared.

Adrienne looked deep into his eyes before whispering her response.

"Magical."

David tapped the arm of his chair. At any moment, the door would open and in would come the sworn enemy of all students of the Academy. *What if he will not teach me? What if he makes Adrienne promise not to teach me?* As if his thoughts had been audible, Adrienne calmed his fears with a touch of her hand. He took her hand and gazed into her beautiful green eyes. *What if I am cast out of Loredana and*

60

I never teach Adrienne philosophy? David had not thought about philosophy for some time. Wrapped up in Adrienne and all she had shown him, it seemed to have fallen by the wayside. A pang echoed through his heart again. A knowledge that something was wrong, or perhaps missing. The fear that he would be a failure. His thoughts were interrupted by the opening door.

David rose from his chair as Adrienne ran and embraced the man who entered. Everything about him reeked of deception and entertainment. He stood tall, with dark features, sporting a cape that dramatized his every move. But what captured David's attention was the magician's wand.

It had been forged in the darkest shade of metal and held significant weight, yet the Master moved it with apparent ease. As a philosopher, David had only heard tell of the object. Legend said that, after leaving the Academy, the Master Magician had crafted a stick which contained all of his magic: a scepter, a symbol of dominance over the path he had chosen to take.

"This must be David," the man said, acknowledging David. Adrienne introduced them.

"I've heard a lot about you," the Master began. "I hear you would like to learn magic?"

"Yes, sir."

"But you are also a philosopher?"

"I am," David felt his pulse begin to race.

The master laughed. "Excellent, that will save time."

"It's not a problem?" David asked, confused.

"Of course not. Some of the best magicians started off as philosophers. Take myself, for instance. The better one understands truth and how it works, the better one may learn to mask it and deceive people. All in good fun, of course."

David laughed in disbelief. He had worried for nothing. The Master shook his hand and told him to be with

Adrienne at her next training session. Impressed by the man's ability to make complete strangers feel as though they were old friends, David could see the Master Magician was a fine blend of style and finesse. The Master apologized to Adrienne for the brevity of his visit, claiming his presence was required elsewhere. With a flick of his wrist, a bouquet of flowers appeared, and Adrienne's face lit up. He winked at David before disappearing through the door.

Both David and Adrienne continued their training, under the Master Magician's tutelage. The more they practiced together, the more David forgot the ways of the Academy.

The Magician taught them everything about magic and the arts of deception. He became very pleased with David and sometimes would even refer to David as the "Master".

One night, the Magician came crashing into David's room, waking him from a deep sleep. "Get up! Get up!" the Magician exclaimed. "It's time."

"Time for what?" David grumbled, rolling over in his bed.

"Time to learn," the Magician responded.

"Learn what?" David yawned. "I know all there is to know. You've taught me everything."

"So you think," responded the Magician in disgust.

"Let's face it," said David, sitting up and rubbing his eyes. "You taught me too well. Now you are just upset because I have surpassed you."

"You fool!" The Master Magician hissed, grabbing David by his nightgown and yanking him off his bed. "No student is greater than his master. Make no mistake, boy, you are nothing!"

"Then what is so important? What must you teach me in the dead of night?" David asked, pushing away.

The Magician responded with one whispered word.

"Sorcery."

Over the next few months David's reality changed. The Magician, whom he now knew as the Sorcerer, had hidden so much from him. David had heard of sorcery but never knew how real it was. Magic had turned out to be a bunch of harmless tricks, but there were no tricks in sorcery. It was dark and sinister; and David began to tamper with things better left untouched.

At first, David split his time between Adrienne and the Sorcerer, spending much of each day with Adrienne, playing tricks on or for people, or just enjoying their time together. But the nights belonged to the Sorcerer. Over and over David practiced enchantments and illusions, but in spite of all of his success, it never pleased his master. He only spurred David on, deeper and deeper into the dark arts. The few times David let the allure of sleep reach through his exhaustion, the Sorcerer threatened to find a new apprentice. David devoted more of his time to sorcery, seeing Adrienne less. David became frustrated with himself and his weaknesses, and it drove him to the edge of madness.

"David," Adrienne said again, snapping her fingers.

David looked up. They both stood next the throne. He had been away again, lost somewhere in his own mind. It had been happening often, but he couldn't help it. There was something there inside of him eating him alive. He could not determine what it was, or perhaps remember it. Whatever it was, it was too complex. He had tried for some time to solve the mystery of this darkness that weighed on him like an iron shroud, but it always evaded him.

"David, what is wrong?" Adrienne asked, feeling she

had his attention.

"Nothing," David responded, twisting his scraggly, unkempt beard with a finger.

She had interrupted his thoughts, again, for the sake of a conversation they had had many times. He turned and began to descend the steps, heading for the door, preferring isolation to confrontation.

"Too busy for me?" she questioned, half teasing, half hurt. She walked to the edge of the first step.

David sighed. When he had first begun learning sorcery he had also begun distancing himself. Adrienne had initially respected his privacy, but David had known it would only be a matter of time before she began to pry. She had never been one to sit idly by. His time was valuable, far too valuable to be wasted on these questions but he knew not answering would only make things worse.

"I'm sorry. What do you want?" he asked, turning back towards her.

Adrienne paused trying to let go of her frustration at his curtness.

"Did you stop loving me?" she asked. "We used to be in love; you used to love my tricks... What happened, David?" a hint of desperation slipped into her voice.

David pressed his fingers against his brow in frustration.

"I don't know. Do we really have to have this conversation, again?" he asked, irritated. "I have things to-" He stopped mid-sentence, looking up to see her now sitting in the throne.

Her face became the stone veil of a practiced princess. She sat still and stoic as a statue, her eyes narrow and empty of emotion as the last of David's echoing words faded away.

"Tell me." She said in a dangerous tone, making it clear this was a demand. "What happened to you?"

David raised his reluctant eyes to meet hers, knowing his words would sting. The Master Magician was the closest thing she had to a father.

"Our Master is teaching me sorcery."

Adrienne's eyes widened.

"How did this come about?" she asked.

"He approached me."

"When?"

David sighed. "Not long after you introduced us."

"I see," she said, considering this information. "Teach me."

For a moment a memory surfaced in David's mind. A vision of the two of them in this same throne room, her requesting he return to teach her. He remembered her bedchamber and his attempt to explain philosophy. A pain spread through his heart. It began sharp like an arrow but then lingered like a poison. He felt sick at the memory.

Answering the Princess's command, he whispered a spell and held out his hand. A tiny dot appeared and began to grow rapidly. He shut his hand before any could escape.

"Is that dark energy?" asked Adrienne, with a curious look in her eyes.

"Yes." David answered. "It's the latest thing I have been working on."

"Why did you stop?"

"I can't control it yet."

As Adrienne rose and walked towards him they both heard the sound. How they heard it they did not know for it couldn't have been any louder than a drop of water tapping the surface of a lake. But they both heard it and looked to the floor.

A single drop of the amorphous substance had slipped out from between David's fingers and landed on the stone floor, erupting, with a tiny splash.

A look of horror washed over David's face and he wasted no time rushing back up the steps to Adrienne and grabbing her by the hand.

65

"We have to go!" he shouted, his eyes shifting towards the door only to find it was too late.

The dark energy looked like a thick ink and moved as an army of determined ants. It rushed to the edges of the room then began to swirl as it moved inwards and climbed each step toward the center like a serpent.

"We are trapped!" Adrienne cried as David pulled her closer to him. They stood in the center of the throne room, watching in terror as the black ooze began to climb towards them.

"David, do something!" She pleaded.

"I… I can't," answered David, watching in disbelief. he and Adrienne stood on the small circular platform as the dark energy enveloped the rest of the floor. It reached up the walls like hands stretching for the top of a cage, consuming and spreading until even the ceiling was covered.

"Do you love me?" he asked, not knowing where the question had come from.

"Yes," she answered, tears beginning to fill her eyes.

"I'm so sorry," he said. "I don't want to hurt you." The words called to mind the memory of the first magic trick they had ever performed together.

"You can't," whispered Adrienne. But David knew he could hurt her, he had, he was hurting her.

"I love you," he whispered.

All of the memories of their time together began to flood his mind and tears fell from his eyes. He remembered the Red Raven Tavern and their first kiss. He remembered the first trick she had shown him in the gardens. He remembered the first time they met when he had just arrived in the city. He remembered why he had come to Loredana and why he had chosen to stay. He kissed her again.

"I was wrong," he whispered, wrapping her in his arms.

Like a flare, a blinding light cut through everything,

expelling the dark energy with a sound that left David's ears ringing. One moment they had been standing embracing each other and the next they were on the floor, staring up at both a bright creature and the Sorcerer. David and Adrienne watched, terrified, yet in awe, as the mystical battle began. Neither could close their eyes, but both felt they were witnessing something not meant for them to know.

David awoke in his old room at the Academy. He blinked once, then twice, then sat up, looking around for an explanation. He slid his feet onto the familiar stone floor. One of his old robes had been laid out on the desk before him. He picked it up with a forgotten reverence. It felt so odd and yet so familiar as he rubbed a section of the fabric between his fingers. He draped the garment over his body, letting the hood fall to his back. *Is it really that simple?* he wondered. *Can I just take it back as though I never left?* He looked over his room, examining every detail. The bare stone walls didn't seem so bare anymore. He knew every crack and blemish on them. He ran his hand over the smooth wood of the flat, un-cushioned bed. This room, this sanctuary, had been his home. The sound of the great bell brought tears to his eyes, and he wept at the bittersweet experience.

A quiet knock on the door pulled David from his thoughts and he wiped the tears from his eyes. He crossed the room and opened the door to find Christopher waiting.

"It's good to have you back," Christopher said, embracing his friend.

"I'm sorry," David offered.

"It's okay, we always knew I was the smarter one," Christopher replied, trying to lighten the mood.

David laughed before asking, "What happened? The last thing I remember I had..."

He stopped, not wanting to tell Christopher about the things he had done.

"The porter found you two mornings ago at the door of the Academy," Christopher stated. "The Masters wanted to send me to the nearest town to ask for the news, but I wanted to stay here in case you woke up. So they sent a runner."

Christopher paused. "People are saying that one of the Ancient appeared in Loredana." He looked to David.

"There was a creature," David began, the horrible event flashing back to his mind. "It was so bright."

"They say an Ancient only appears when there is threat of a great evil." Christopher commented. "No one has seen one in centuries."

David sat on the edge of his bed, taking it all in.

"Where is Adrienne?" David asked.

"You were the only one found at the door," Christopher answered.

"I'm leaving," David said to Christopher as they ate lunch together.

"But you just returned," Christopher replied.

It was true. It had been several days since David had awoken in the Academy, but he knew he could not stay. From the moment his eyes had opened, Adrienne had been on his mind. She would visit him in dreams, reopening his wounds with her trick knife. He had even tried Christopher's suggestion to write to her, knowing she would never see his words. He had written pages and pages, remembering, questioning, and apologizing. There had only been a few moments since his return that he had managed to forget. Then someone would sound a little like her or even look like her at a quick glance and it would all come racing back to him. She had become his mind's prisoner or perhaps his mind had become hers.

David sighed. "I've tried to reclaim my life as a philosopher. I really have. But everything is different now."

Christopher looked at him, debating whether or not he should say what he was thinking.

"Speak freely," David said.

"You know you can't return to her."

David nodded, pain flashing through his eyes. Christopher hadn't said this as a command. David could return to Loredana; the Academy would not interfere. Both knew in their hearts if David returned, he and Adrienne would eventually revert to their old ways, and in the end David would do more harm than good.

"I know," he answered.

"You love her," Christopher said.

"I do."

They continued their meal in silence for a while.

"So what will you do?" Christopher asked. "Where will you go?"

All his life he had searched for the truth. He wanted to know it and to live by it. He knew he could never be with Adrienne. But he had to see her.

David looked at his food, but made no effort to eat.

"I miss her," he said. "I have to know she's safe."

"What if she's not?" Christopher asked, concerned. "Will you intervene?"

David felt as if they were standing on the bridge all over again, and he rose from his seat.

"I never apologized to you for the way I left things."

"You never needed to," Christopher replied, rising as well.

"I was wrong," David continued. "You were right; I can't save her. I can only point her in the right direction. Then, it's up to her."

Christopher gave him a quizzical look.

"It doesn't have to be this way, David."

"I know," David answered, as the noon bell rang.

Christopher smiled a sad smile and nodded. They embraced for the final time.

David climbed to the top of the great mountain and broke his oath to the truth once more. The wind rose and the mountain quaked beneath him. Using only white magic, he broke the mountain's summit and carried it into the sky. Higher and higher, he rose until he could see not just Loredana but the whole world. From the stars he watches his beloved, shining bright flares, desperately trying to guide her to the truth. To this day, he remains there, isolated from all he once loved, alone for all eternity. That is the legend of Polaris, the legend of the North Star.

THE PRICE OF BEAUTY

3

I look like I'm dead, the Princess thought to herself. *I should be dead.* Cassandra lay on the floor of the octagonal room, looking at her reflection in the mirrored walls. She hated her reflection, and no matter where she turned she could not escape it. It echoed a voice from her past she could never be rid of. It was the incarnation of her curse. *"You are a foolish child. Beauty will not gain you love. But so that you may learn, I shall grant you the gift of its curse."* Those were the haunting words the enchantress had spoken.

For centuries Cassandra had contemplated those words. Immortality, eternal youth, and eternal beauty had been bestowed upon her by the enchantress. Everyone had stared at her, the men with desire, the women with hatred, as though she were a goddess or perhaps a monster. Cassandra had often wondered if they even saw her at all. She had wanted to shrink, to become so small and insignificant no one would notice her, to slip away from the world and all existence. Wars had been threatened for her hand in marriage, and so the King had locked his daughter in a tower. He swore if any man could climb to the top they could have his daughter's hand. No one had come.

Her beauty would never permit her to be loved, she knew that now. Cassandra rose, standing inches away from the mirror, watching as she ran her fingers down her cheek. Everything about her appearance revolted her, and she often wondered if she really was beautiful. *I should be dead,* she thought to herself. *I should be dead.*

The thought of returning home weighed on Alexander as he stood in the outer courtyard of the castle, waiting to be permitted into the King's chambers. Having no home to return to, this was the closest thing he would ever experience. The city of Omines stood on the edge of a cliff overlooking the ocean. He had been here only once before, when he had been very young, but he knew most of the city's stories. Many nights of Alexander's childhood had been spent at the local tavern of his hometown, sitting alongside his father, listening to an older generation reminisce of their great adventures. His father had been a great storyteller, and he often spoke of this ancient city. He had once saved the life of its King, starting an unorthodox but intimate friendship. Alexander had vague memories of his father introducing him to the King. Now he waited to be introduced to him again. Why after all this time had the King summoned him? Alexander had several theories. None of them was pleasant.

Upon entering the city, Alexander had felt as though he had become the specter in some long forgotten fairy tale. The winter snow carried a bewitching effect as each delicate flake fell, blanketing the city in visual purity. Children too naive to recognize the dangers of sickness ran about trying to catch snowflakes. Was it foolishness or mere innocence?

As he stood in the palace courtyard, he studied the two guards who detained him. It was no mystery to them Alexander was not royalty. His sandy blonde hair was shaggy but not long enough to hide his face. A tattered and faded blue-gray cape hung off his right shoulder, covering the mark he bore on his arm. Scuffed leather armor protected his chest but still permitted a good range of motion. His body stood tall and lean. Nonetheless, his appearance still witnessed to his strength. The soldiers could see he was a warrior but not a soldier like them. Alexander observed their thick steel-plated armor.

"He is ready," said one of the King's personal guards, poking his head out from a side door.

Alexander followed the guard through a series of passages.

The King's private chambers had been arranged to mimic his throne room, with a chair at the end of his bed and a warming fire in the hearth. The first thing Alexander noticed was the stench, and it confirmed his suspicion. Death wears perfume, and the King was soaked in it. He sat in an elaborate oak chair, his withered hands curled tight over its armrests. His gaunt face looked up, and he watched Alexander through sunken, swollen eyes. What little bits of fragmented hair he had left had gone white with age or anxiety. Alexander had been around violence so long he had almost forgotten what natural death looked like.

The King's advisors stood at a distance where the King could not see them, speaking in whispers and hushed tones. Alexander ignored the vultures as he stepped forward into the King's gaze.

"Alexander," the King spoke softly. "You have grown."

"My King, it is an honor," Alexander replied.

"Am I still King?" he asked, looking away as if he could somehow see the horizon through the stone walls of his chambers. "These days I feel so awful, it's difficult to remember I'm still a man."

"Allow me to remind you," Alexander said, bowing low.

"You are so much like your father. He would be very proud of the man you have become."

Alexander felt a pang of grief in his heart. He had often wondered what his father would have thought of his journey to manhood. He answered, "Thank you, my King."

"All sons make mistakes, and all fathers love them in

spite of their flaws," the King offered, sensing Alexander's hesitation. He paused before switching subjects. "I know this journey must not have been an easy one. I can never tell you how much it means to me."

"You summoned me," Alexander replied.

The King sighed. "I must ask a great deal of you. There is an army coming. They will destroy our lands and raze the city. It is no secret I am dying, and my son is…young and impressionable. He is in no way ready to defend the city from a force like this. He needs a guide. Your father and I once defended your homeland; and though this was never your home, I must now ask you to do the same."

The King bowed his head in shame. Alexander watched as the advisors shared looks of disapproval and spite.

"Who is coming?" Alexander asked.

"The savage," the King replied.

Alexander knew of whom the King spoke.

Cain.

The Prince awoke, his heart racing. Sleep had liberated him from the unbearable questions which plagued his mind, but now sleep abandoned him. He had been dreaming again, though he often referred to his dreams as nightmares. He had dreamt of her, and he knew his mind would be a slave to her for the better half of his day.

He got up from his bed and made his way through his room to the table. Though no one would ever guess, he possessed one of the largest rooms in the castle. Blankets of animal skins lay strewn about, not only to decorate his bed but to prevent the cold, which seemed to be the very essence of the stone floor. Artwork stood propped up on makeshift frames around the room, creating the illusion he lived in a sort of a maze. On the table sat a basin of water his servants had left for him. Next to the basin lay a wedge of cheese and a plate of assorted fruits which were on the verge of expiration. The servants had also left several candles scattered about the table and his room to provide a dim light. He stared at the basin for a moment, watching the shards of ice that had formulated overnight float about, before dipping his hands in and splashing the frigid liquid on his face. Not even the coldest water would wash his mind clean of the dream or, more specifically, of her.

He had been twelve years old when he had first heard the legend: the legend that the city he was destined to rule possessed the most beautiful woman ever known to man. That's when the dreams had begun, and his dreams were the closest he would ever be to her. They had begun as the face of a woman, then conversations, but as the years passed something had changed. Now, she would come to him in tears. "Why?" she would ask him. He could not bear to see her tears. He wanted to comfort her. He wanted to tell her. He would reach for her, only to find he was reaching through empty air. One moment he was there and the next he was not. He was falling. The Prince trembled at the thought.

After drying his face and clothing himself more appropriately for the temperature, the Prince began to maneuver through the chaotic mess towards his desk. Clusters of paints and charcoal cluttered the edges of his workstation like ornaments on a shrine. Parchments with his sketches, of varying degrees of completion, adorned the center of the table with the face of his obsession. He gazed at his most recent sketch.

The sound of a servant approaching made him look up from his work.

"What is it?" he asked.

"He has come, Prince Silas," the servant stated.

"Where is he now?" Silas asked, still staring at his work.

"In the training yard, I believe."

Silas dismissed him.

After several more minutes the Prince rose and left for the training yard. He passed through a large network of hallways and corridors until he arrived at a small wooden door that led into the soldiers' barracks. Silas opened the door and crossed the threshold into a long hallway with rooms on either side. Each room had two beds, two desks, and two sets of shelves, one set on each side of the room. His father had brought him to the barracks as a child. The hallway had seemed much longer then. Every bed had been made, every piece of armor polished and ready, as though they themselves were soldiers. It had been pristine. If not for the few personal items on the shelves and desks, it had been hard to imagine anyone actually lived there. He averted his eyes from the rooms he passed now. The unkempt manner in which the soldiers conducted themselves had led to the disheveled state of their living quarters. The city had fallen so far.

As he reached the far side of the barracks, the Prince heard the soldiers in a commotion. They seemed unsettled. The door at the far end of the barracks stood open. It led to a terrace, which overlooked the soldiers' training ground. The training ground consisted of a row of targets for archery practice, ten targets in length. There was a forge in the back where the soldiers could equip themselves with and repair armor. And in the center was a hand-to-hand and weapons training circle the soldiers often called "the pit."

The men were silent as the Prince stepped out onto the terrace, but the silence was not for him. The Prince had never seen so many of the city's soldiers at the same time. Not even at the annual city festival when the soldiers put on a special parade and show for the King. Hundreds of men stood waiting, watching, their eyes locked on one figure. He stood in the pit. *Alexander.*

"I understand your concerns," Alexander continued his address to the men. "I am a foreigner here, but my father fought alongside your King many years ago. I come to you today by the King's request. We will train together, and together we shall prevail. If any of you should question my command, let him step into the ring with me now."

The Prince could not help but smile at Alexander's speech. He was not the greatest orator the Prince had ever heard, but he had spoken with honesty and authority. This was his power play. The Prince could not help but wonder if this man could deliver.

One at a time, several men stepped into the ring and one at a time Alexander beat them. He moved through combat with a grace the Prince had never seen. He was not a brute who depended on strength alone. Every motion he made was swift and deliberate. The Prince watched, recalling his father's words. *Fighting is like a dance, a dance with death.* This man must have courted death for years. It was the only way he could have learned the dance so well. With or without weapons, it was clear Alexander would be the victor.

The men watched, jeering at each other, goading one another to be the next contestant. It did not take long before the challenges ceased. Alexander had won the respect of his men.

The Prince watched him waiting in the ring. Confident. Patient. Beads of sweat hung off of his hair, several escaping down his face. His breath remained steady. He was tired, but by no means exhausted.

A marking on his right shoulder caught the attention of the Prince. It depicted a soldier's helmet on the hilt of a sword. The sword had been planted in the ground and a cape wrapped around it. Not many men knew its significance, but the Prince did.

There had been stories of a Legion, an elite fighting

81

force. After each battle they would bury their enemies, leaving their equipment to mark their grave. The Legion had been undefeatable. Many years ago, after a great battle, they had disappeared. They had vanished and were never heard from again.

The Prince descended the stairs onto the training grounds. As he stepped into the pit to face Alexander, a hush fell over the men as if he had cast a spell. They watched like statues, in silence and awe of the impending duel. After a moment of eying one another, the Prince broke the silence.

"So you are the one my father has chosen to lead our army," he said, examining Alexander. "Why are you here, training the army of a city doomed to fall?"

Whispers of Cain's name could be heard passing through the troops.

"Your father asked for my help," Alexander answered.

"The people believe my father is a very wise king, but the elders disagree. They feel he has become desperate in his sickness." The Prince motioned to a nearby soldier for two swords. "What do you believe?" the Prince asked, handing one to Alexander.

"I guess we are going to find out," he replied.

The silence broke and the soldiers began to rage, yelling, cheering, and placing bets. The Prince moved first, lunging at Alexander, and so the dance began. Every move the Prince made Alexander countered with ease. It was as if he could anticipate his opponent's every move. The Prince had been wrong about this man. Alexander had not courted death; he was death. In spite of all of Silas' effort he could not help but wonder if this man was going easy on him. Then, seeing an opening, the Prince took it, and in one swift motion disarmed Alexander. The fight was over.

"You are one of the most gifted fighters I have ever encountered," the Prince said.

"Thank you, my Prince."

"My name is Silas. And you, Alexander, shall lead the city's army." He turned to leave. "Meet me in my chambers when you have finished with the men."

"If I could only have one woman in my life, I would choose you." Cassandra could still hear the words. The first time she had heard them they had branded themselves onto her heart. Her father had said them, but not to her. Those words had been for the daughter of a visiting nobleman. Cassandra could still recall the young woman's face, eyes full of mirth and mystery, encased by long dark hair. Her scarlet lips had locked into place with the King's as he kissed her passionately. Cassandra's father had not known she was there, but she had been a silent witness to it all. At the time Cassandra believed her father had loved the girl. Why else would he have said such things to her? But as she grew older, she learned why she had never seen the nobleman's daughter after that night.

Now the words came to the forefront of her mind once more.

Cassandra giggled, as she took a step backward and looked at her toes.

"I know it's silly, but would you dance with me?" she asked.

Silence.

"Okay," she whispered and held up her hand to meet her partner's, as was customary in the Omines tradition. She had always been a marvelous dancer, even as a child. As their dance came to a close she could sense she was going to be kissed. She closed her eyes and waited, imagining what it would be like. Lost in the moment. She opened her eyes and saw only herself in the mirrors. Her imaginary friend was gone.

She lay down on the floor and stared up at the ceiling. Its bare surface was the only place she did not have to face her horrid reflection. She thought about her imaginary friend and began to ponder. Who had the worse fate? Living in eternal torment or fading into oblivion?

Alexander followed the guards to the Prince's chambers. He had put up a good fight in the ring so as to keep the men's respect. He had lost the fight to protect Silas's reputation. Silas was a practiced fighter but Alexander was a seasoned warrior. After their match he had dismissed the men, cleaned himself up, and joined them for dinner.

As the guards announced him and he entered the Prince's chambers, he was surprised to find the room filled with art. He had seen rooms decorated with tributes to the greatness of their creator, but this was different. Alexander gazed at each piece, allowing himself to become immersed within the images. He let his eyes pass over them, unveiling the stories being portrayed and letting them come to life, almost feeling as if he were reliving someone else's memory. Pigments and paints, small lumps of charcoals, and chunks of mosaic tiles lay strewn about. Hundreds of portraits had been arranged, all different sizes, shapes, and mediums. Many of them were completed, while others were designed only to accentuate or practice certain features. Though they were all beautiful, every piece was of the same woman, which disturbed Alexander. As he approached the Prince, who continued to work on his present painting, Alexander recollected the story of a painter, which he had heard many years before.

There had been a painter who had painted the portrait of a beautiful woman, a stranger who had visited his shop. Days passed, and she did not return. The painter began to stare at the portrait, imagining what she was like; kind, beautiful, yet mysterious. He dreamed of her, longing for her. He fixated on all the flaws in his portrait, furious he had not mimicked God's creation better. He painted her portrait again and again, and she became an unachievable torment to him. The painter grew to be a bitter, old, unhappy man.

Years later, a woman came to his shop and purchased the portrait. The painter told her he would have given anything to have known her name. The woman, turning to leave, told him her name. She had been right in front of him but he had been so lost in his fantasy, he had not recognized her.

Alexander watched and admired the Prince's skill, as he finished the lady's golden hair, which fell in loose waves down the edges of a perfectly crafted jawline. Her crimson lips opened ever so slightly, portraying the illusion she was about to whisper a secret. Alexander found none of her features to be as distracting as her emerald green eyes.

"She's beautiful," Alexander commented as he joined the Prince near his work.

"The likes of whom no man has seen in centuries," the Prince answered, setting down his brush.

"Who is she?" Alexander asked, with a gesture towards the painting.

"Have you not heard the legend?" Silas asked in surprise. "Centuries ago, the King of Omines had a daughter. As a child, she begged an enchantress to make her beautiful. The enchantress gifted her with eternal life, eternal youth, and an unnatural beauty.

"This pleased the King. He took pride in his daughter, throwing many parties and bragging about her gifts. It was not long before the whole world had heard of this girl." Silas stepped away from the painting, motioning for Alexander to join him at the window.

"As she matured, so did her beauty. Every man and every king became enamored with the thought of her, and the threat of a world war surfaced. Upon realizing this, her father confined her to the castle, but it did not end there. He knew he had to dispose of her. He ordered a tower erected and locked his daughter away," Silas said, pointing to the tower which rose up from the center of the city.

"He swore if any man could ascend the tower from the outside, he could have the Princess's in marriage. Many men tried the climb, but none prevailed. After several years and hundreds of deaths, people began to forget about the Princess and her beauty," Silas ended his story.

"Many don't understand the price of beauty. Those who have it often believe it defines their worth, and those who desire it can be led to something truly hideous," Alexander said, after brief reflection.

"So which are you?" Silas teased. "The beautiful, or the seeker of beauty?"

"Neither, anymore," Alexander answered. "What about you? Why your fascination with her?" He tried to be generous by not calling it an obsession.

A smile broke across the Prince's face as he asked, "Alexander, do you believe in destiny?"

Alexander nodded.

"They say I am destined for greatness, and when fate puts something right in front of you…isn't it obvious?" Silas nodded towards the window and the tower beyond.

"I saw a door at the base of the tower," Alexander stated.

"It locks from the inside." Silas answered. "We presume it is for whoever makes it to the top. So they will not have to climb down."

"Have you ever attempted the climb?" Alexander asked.

"No," The Prince answered, a troubled look coming over him. "My father would not permit it. He believes the legend is silly and dangerous. I am my father's only heir... much too valuable to be lost to the tower."

"There is wisdom in your father's words," Alexander replied.

"Unfortunately," Silas muttered, accustomed to this response. "Forgive me for earlier," he said, changing topics and moving away from the window. "I had to know you were committed to the cause. The city depends on it. I saw the mark on your right shoulder when you were training the men. You were a Legionary."

A fog fell over Alexander's eyes.

Silas poured two glasses of wine, handing one to Alexander. He swirled the dark liquid in his glass as he continued.

"Last I knew, the warriors the Legion trained were impossible to stop. So am I to believe you are out of practice or that you let me win?"

Alexander said nothing.

"I thought so." Silas said, sipping his wine. "I have heard rumors of the enemy who approaches. They say he is an unstoppable savage who cannot be reasoned with. He brings nations to their knees. Tell me, Alexander, you are a warrior, but do you believe you can train the army to withstand a warlord?"

"I know without me, you won't."

Silas finished his wine, remaining neutral to Alexander's response. He dismissed Alexander and returned to his most recent portrait.

As Alexander approached the door, he looked back for a moment with one last question. "The girl in the tower... What's her name?"

"I wish I knew," Silas answered.

Within the month Alexander created an army. He kept the men on a rigorous training schedule. He knew they would never be Legionaries, but he would settle for soldiers. He didn't want them broken, he wanted them ready. He did everything alongside them: eating, sleeping, and the constant running. When Alexander had first joined the Legion he had hated running. It had been difficult and painful. Most nights he had gone to bed wondering if it would be better to cut his legs off than to endure another day of the torture. In the end, running had saved him.

He spent time with each of the men, one by one, in the pit, making sure they were ready for single combat. Most were not, but after several rounds in the pit each learned to hold his own. He ran them through mock sieges, training them in strategies of defending the castle walls. He put them under intense pressure. But it is in pressure that diamonds are made. He had started with coal, and now he had diamonds, sharp diamonds.

Training ceased for three days at the announcement of the King's passing. Shops closed, the soldiers were dismissed, and the city sank into mourning. The King's body was placed on a pyre, and after respects were paid, he was purified by fire for the afterlife.

Alexander continued running the men until the day the lookout came for him.

"The enemy will be here tomorrow," said the soldier.

Time seemed to stop.

"And we shall be ready."

Silas stood at the edge of the top of the legendary tower, looking down on the city below. His father had loved Omines, and now his father was gone. His beloved city was as he was now; fatherless.

"Why?" he heard her ask from behind him. He didn't want to turn to face her, but he was powerless. There she stood before him, the angel who haunted him like a ghost, her ocean eyes releasing rivers of tears. Silas had never decided what was worse; the knowledge of what would come, or the knowledge that he could not stop it.

"Why?" she begged. "Why did you leave me here?"

They stood; silent, motionless. Silas could feel his heart pounding. The question seemed to echo in his ears. He had walked away from the tower so many times, and every time he had been walking away from her. The truth had become unbearable, and it crushed him like a weight. He could have climbed the tower years ago, and years ago, he had desired to. Perhaps it had been his father's words of caution, or maybe he had just grown to be a coward. Either way, a small sliver of despair had sunk into the Prince's heart like a fish hook, but instead of pulling him up, it dragged him down into the depths and the darkness.

"Because," he began. The air seemed to leave his lungs and he felt as though his very soul was leaving with it. "Because I was afraid."

She turned away and he reached for her, but it was too late. He was falling. Faster and faster, he fell.

Silas's eyes flashed open, a cold sweat soaking his body. He had fallen asleep on his father's throne. He rose, disturbed, and began to pace the long rectangular throne room. Three pillars stood on either side of him, six in total, behind which were the mosaic-covered walls. A fire pit in the center provided the room with heat, though the fire burned low. Lost in his thoughts, he wandered through the space.

Confident he was alone, Silas turned back to his father's former seat. He knelt down, feeling it would respect his father's memory, the only thing the chair now possessed. "Father, forgive me," he began, approaching as if his father were still there or could somehow still hear him. "I am afraid." Silence answered his words; and although he had grown accustomed to the same response from his father, this silence felt much deeper and resonated within him.

Their relationship had been strained, but in his father's final moments Silas had stood by his side. It had been too late to rehash the old arguments and emotions, as his father had lost the ability to speak and most of his consciousness. Silas tried to remember their last conversation, but he could not.

The King was dead, and a warlord approached the city even as Silas mourned. The city seemed to be an infant left on a mountaintop to brave the elements. The responsibility of the throne towered over him, and Silas closed his eyes as he heard his small tears kiss the stone floor. He no longer knelt; he crumbled.

Had his father ever had any faith in him? This was not the first tower Silas had faced. He had been fourteen the first time he told his father of his desire to make the climb. Not only had the King refused to let him, but he added doubt to his son's dream, asking the boy, "Even supposing you did make it, what if she is a witch? Not a princess. What is she is actually trapped and you ended up releasing her?"

Silas' dreams had been like a beautiful tapestry, and his father had unraveled every strand to try to make something of his own. His father had undercut his desire to be a warrior as well, saying, "To prepare for war is to invite it. Politics! Politics and negotiations, that is what I shall teach you." Silas had ignored his words and trained with the palace guard. But as soon as the threat of Cain arose, his father had called Alexander.

Silas rose. He passed by the throne and pushed through two giant doors which led to a terrace. The cool twilight air rushed to greet him. He walked to the rail and looked out over the ocean, breathing the salt air and listening to the waves lapping far below. It was almost peaceful. His father had been a king of peace, and now Silas found himself faced with a time of war. He felt empty and unprepared, as if he had dreamt of everything and accomplished nothing. He wondered if his father had had dreams. If he had, he must have given up on them long before Silas was born.

"Cain's army approaches…How am I to defend a city?" he asked, looking out to the night sky. "If Cain conquers us, he will burn this place to the ground and leave the people to the dogs. I'm sorry, father… I want my legacy to be more than ash and bones."

Alexander sat perched on the wall of the city, waiting with patience for what the following morning would bring. Silas, whom he had not seen since the King's funeral, joined him on the wall. With the death of the King and the impending siege, Alexander didn't have to guess whether Silas had a lot on his mind. They sat in silence until Silas broke the peace.

"I heard they have arrived."

"Just beyond the ridge," Alexander answered, motioning to the distance.

"Alexander, where were you when my father's men came for you?"

"In a tavern."

"That's not what I meant."

"You meant what happened to me after the Legion?"

Alexander continued to stare out into the darkness. He was a simple man, who did not enjoy reflecting on the past. He had done that for too long. He had come to believe the past should not be forgotten, but it should not rule one's future. He did not enjoy telling his own story, but Silas had a right to know.

"My father lived the life of a soldier. When I was a

boy, I did not see him often, but I loved my father. I wanted to be just like him: a man of glory, honor, and danger. When I was old enough I joined the Seventh Legion. I wanted to make him proud. I learned war was nothing like he or his friends had discussed. I saw and did many gruesome and cruel things. I found very little glory and even less honor. Eventually, the Legion took on a force too strong, and we were defeated. I ran like a coward and they hunted me, until a woman named Saoirse, who lived in the woods, hid me from them. I stayed with her for years, for she was quite beautiful.

"One day a prince sent for her. I sat alone in her absence, and in the silence I heard faint voices. I thought I was hearing things and ignored it, but in time I realized it was coming from a hole behind the house. The hole led to a cave, and in the cave was a tiny metal box. 'Where are you?' I called. 'In here,' they replied. 'We are fairies and the witch trapped us in here. Please, sir, help free us and we, in turn, shall help free you.' At this point, Saoirse returned, and she asked what I was doing. I told her I had heard voices. She kissed me and assured me no one was there.

"Months went by, and I could not help but wonder. So, one night, I returned to the box in the cave, sitting with it, listening. I could bear it no longer. I threw open the lid, expecting nothing to happen. The room was illuminated by the light of thousands of fairies. They swarmed and they sang all through the room. As they moved, I noticed whatever they touched changed. I saw the cave was filled with books, tools, and substances for practicing the dark arts. Saoirse found me and screamed, transforming into a hideous old witch. She attacked but the fairies brought me my sword, and with their help I defeated her.

"I ran again, ashamed and disgusted. I continued to run for years. Until I stumbled upon a tavern where I was given an offer to face my past. I decided it was time to face my demons, not run from them."

Alexander stood in silence. The night seemed to have gotten colder. Silas reviewed the story in his mind.

"Do you think we stand a chance against Cain?" he asked, as though they were partners in a game of dice.

"Go rest, Silas. You're going to need it."

Silas nodded as Alexander began to walk off into the night.

"Wait! Who conquered the Legion?" Silas called, but Alexander was gone.

The night dragged on, but Alexander could not sleep. He remembered how excitement had kept him up before his first battle, and how after he had never truly slept again. He had inspected the castle walls and talked with sentries. He now walked through the streets until he found himself at the base of the legendary tower. He could not explain what drew him to the tower, but he had gone. It looked as though it touched the sky. He reached for it but hesitated before touching it, as if it were a sacred vessel of some sort, or as if by touching it he would somehow contact the woman trapped inside it. He scoffed at his own ridiculousness, grabbed the smooth cool stone, found a handhold, and began to climb. Arm over arm, he pulled himself higher. He made good progress until a small piece of rock broke under his foot. Alexander slipped and braced himself as his body smashed up against the rock wall. He looked down as he tried to adjust his footing. He had risen much higher than he had thought. He continued to climb, resolving not to look down again. As he neared the top, the climb began taking its toll. His arms were sore, but he knew there was no turning back. He could see the ledge. At the top of the tower there was an octagonal structure made of glass. There was just enough of a rim for a man to stand on and carefully walk around. Alexander took a deep breath and looked for the next handhold, but the rock went smooth. His muscles strained to keep him against the wall. He reached up, but it was useless. He shifted his weight, trying to let his muscles relax. He looked over his shoulder as the first rays of the sun peeked over the horizon. "This is it," he whispered to himself, as he let go of the wall, and lunged up towards the ledge.

She had been poisoned by her own request. The poison had spread through her, but instead of condemning her to death, it cursed her to immortal life. It had contaminated her with the features of a goddess, forever ostracizing her from humanity.

Cassandra often dreamt of what could have happened if her father had not built the tower. She could have left, ran away to the far edge of the earth. She could have married, not a king, but a poor farmer. They would not live in a castle but in the most remote area of the world. She would captivate him, and he would love her. But how could a man love a goddess? No, he would use her. She would not be his goddess but his charm, his talisman. Then they would come for her, and there would be war, death, and destruction.

Cassandra awoke from her nightmare, upset as always. Her body felt numb and cold. It was as if another lifetime had been ripped from her and cast into the fires of hell. She was wrong to dream; the tower was safer. It was the only way she could protect humanity, the only way she could protect herself. Picking herself up off of the floor, she watched her reflection in the mirror. With brisk steps she approached it as though it were an enemy. "I hate you!" she screamed, driving her fist into the image. She almost laughed as she felt the skin on her hand split. The mirror cracked like a spider's web and fell into a thousand pieces. She looked down at the fractured reflection of her face. Her long dark hair, her skin, and those sad eyes, which had once held so much life. *There I am*, she thought. A drop of dark red blood distracted her as it fell from her hand. There would be no scars. Before the tower she had tried so many times to taint or mar her beauty, but it was all in vain. She had thrown away her purity, but her father had been quick to put a stop to that. Not so much for her, but for the family name. Confined in her room, her first prison, she had cut herself only to watch her skin heal before the bleeding had stopped. No one who saw her would ever know the hundreds of scars she bore beneath her skin. She picked up a shard of the mirror, embracing the temptation once more. That is when she saw him. In front of her, in the space where the mirror had been, stood a man. At first she was afraid, until she realized between them stood a transparent wall of glass. *How long has he been there?* she wondered, approaching with caution.

"Who are you?" she whispered.

The man continued to stare.

"Who are you!" she shouted at him, once again angry and afraid. The man didn't flinch. He placed his hand on the glass wall and tapped it with his fingers. Cassandra reached out and put her hand up against his. A solid inch divided them. She looked at his eyes; they were fixated on her. He lowered his eyes to the shard of mirror in her hand. She dropped it, embarrassed. He looked back at her. *What is it?* She thought.

"What?" she whispered to the glass. He produced a dagger. Cassandra took a step back before remembering the barrier between them. She stared in disbelief as the man took the blade and slowly slid it across his shoulder. She wanted to stop him. He dipped his finger into the blood and wrote on the glass. She shook her head, unable to understand. *The fool, he doesn't realize it is backward on my side.* When he finished he pointed to the mirror behind her. She turned and saw what he had written. *You are lovable and worthy of being loved.* She turned back to him, but he was gone.

The morning light ran across the ice-crusted snow, reflecting into the eyes of the watchman. He stared out into the distance, squinting, searching for anything that might betray the enemy position. Then he heard horns, and the enemy poured over the hill. The watchman raised the alarm.

Alexander thought about what had just transpired as he walked through the streets back towards his post. He had made it to the top of the tower and found himself face to face with the most beautiful young woman he had ever seen. She sat imprisoned in a room where the walls were made of mirrors. Behind each mirror was an inch of glass for support. He had seen her through the brokenness, and she had seen him. Her eyes had spoken all of her secrets. He had told her what he wished someone had told him so many years ago. Then he had left through a spiral stairwell that descended on the inside wall of the tower.

His thoughts were interrupted by a messenger who ran up shouting, "Sir! Sir! Come quickly!"

"Are they approaching?" Alexander asked. "Are they at the walls?"

"No Sir, they've breached the main gate!"

Alexander drew his sword and was already running before the messenger had finished.

As Alexander rounded a corner he saw the enemy had broken their defenses. A handful of Cain's men had taken the ramparts and the gate room, raising the gate for their companions. Alexander's disordered men froze in shock as they watched the enemy begin to pour in like water, rushing through a severed dam.

Alexander charged up the steps onto the wall, dispatching enemies as he went. Soon the city would be overrun. He ducked under an enemy sword and retaliated by slicing the man's throat. He charged for the gate room. The only thing between him and his destination appeared to be a giant with an ax. The man towered over him. Alexander jumped up onto the edge of the wall, launching himself towards his opponent. The man grabbed Alexander before he could strike. He felt the man's fingers lock around his throat. Like lightning Alexander drew his dagger and sliced through the man's inner arm. The giant-like man yelped in pain, and Alexander drove the dagger into the side of the man's neck. The huge man grabbed at his wound before toppling over the snow-covered ledge. Wasting no time, Alexander charged into the gate room, dashing to the release lever for the gate. He pulled it down hard and heard a rumbling followed by a great crash below him. He breathed a sigh of relief. The city would not fall today.

Rage rose from deep within Silas's heart. He had been a fool. Worse, he had been betrayed. Silas had watched the enemy charge the city. He had fought them on the ramparts of the wall. Alexander had not come. The enemy had launched its attack, and in fear Silas had sought out Alexander, who was nowhere to be found. The man who his father had claimed would save the city. He should have stayed on the walls. He should have saved the city himself. When Silas had finally found him, Alexander had been slipping out of the door, the ancient door which had never been opened. The door to the tower. He had been inside and had seen *her*. The enemy battered the gates, and where was the city's hero? Here, stealing the only thing the King had not been able to take from him. Reality set in. His father was dead, and he was alone.

Before Silas could do anything Alexander had disappeared.

Silas sat on his father's throne, brooding. There had to be a way, a way to prove himself. If he could not out-fight Alexander, he would out-think him. His mind fell to the ancient stories his father had made him study, when Silas should have been training to fight. *A lot of good they will do me now*, he thought. They had been stories of warriors, kings, and poets. He sat, his face like stone; until one story surfaced in Silas' mind. A wry smile crept across his face as the gears of his mind began to turn.

The story, commonly known as "The Wordsmith," was one of the darker tales he had ever been taught. The wordsmith was an evil poet, who tricked a great hero into giving up his true love. The poet's words were so sweet and so deceptive. For the hero to get his love back, the wordsmith convinced the hero to give up their firstborn son. Many years later, the poet tricks the son, who returns only to kill his own father. The lesson being men of sweet words must be dealt with cautiously. *Everybody wants something*, was the famous line of the wordsmith. Silas now mulled it over again and again. He wanted the girl in the tower and he wanted to save his legacy. Cain wanted the city, the prestige. But what if there was something else? What else could Cain, the conqueror, possibly want?

Silas rose and called for the Captian of the guard. The Captian arrived and Silas told him, "Relieve Alexander of his post and his armor. Escort him to the prison and await further instruction."

The Captian stood, hesitant.

"Go, or you will join him!" Silas shouted.

Then he summoned a messenger.

Silas, "*the wordsmith*," he thought.

"You called, Sir?" the messenger asked.

"I want you to deliver a message to Cain," Silas said

looking up. "Tell him I have something he wants."

Cursed for eternity: that is how Cassandra had envisioned herself. Condemned by her own words to be forever alone. Now, she found herself plagued by new words, words written in blood. She stood inches away from the glass, no longer fascinated with her own reflection so much as she was with the words of a stranger. *You are loveable and worthy of being loved.* Could he possibly believe that? Or was it merely a lie to win her over? But it was written in blood. His blood.

Cassandra looked down from her tower, watching fire consume the city. It was a plague, spreading with a swiftness and fierceness she had not witnessed for hundreds of years. The glass prevented the sounds of anguished cries from reaching her ears, but it did not ease the horror of the spectacle. Cain's men raced through the gates while hundreds of people fled, their instinct to survive overtaking them. Like ocean waves ramming a ship against the rocks, the enemy destroyed everything in their path, leaving bodies and debris in their wake.

The day Cassandra had been placed in the tower, there had been chaos: riots outside the palace and armies perched outside the city gates. Her people had hated her, cursed her name for bringing trouble to their city. They did not know how or why she had become so beautiful. All they knew was they could not bear it. It had to be tainted or eradicated, but it could not stay. She had not intended any of it. How could she have known the gravity of her request? Now, she watched the fate which had befallen her city, a fate she was in part responsible for.

She traced the letters of his words with her fingers as she began to question; which was the truth and which was the lie?

The bare skin of Alexander's feet rested on the cold stone floor. He had been about to summon the Prince for a council of war when the Captian of the guard came for him with four additional men. They had been torn by their duty. He had not resisted them. He had been stripped of his weapons and armor. His hands were secured tight behind his back with a thick shackle that chafed his skin the more he struggled. He sat waiting in the darkness until what he guessed were the late hours of the day, before a sliver of light pierced the artificial night, growing larger, like a small blade severing a rich fabric. The door opened and eight men entered the room bearing torches: four of the Palace Guard, two of Cain's soldiers, Silas, and Cain. *So he tried to make a deal.* Alexander glared at Silas, who skulked back into the shadows.

A large figure stepped forward. Even in the dim lighting of the torches there was no mistaking him. His hair flowed long and unkempt, like a lion's mane. A necklace of teeth, from the beasts he had killed, decorated his chest. His clothes had been made of animal hides, and he moved as though he were more animal than man.

"Cain," Alexander whispered.

"He bears the mark of the Legion on his arm," Silas offered.

Cain crouched like a cat to Alexander's level. His breath bathed Alexander's face in the stench of rotting animals. Cain's empty eyes seemed to soak up the defiance in Alexander's as they stared at each other. No words were spoken, and none were necessary. After several moments Cain rose. "Kill," he uttered just above a whisper and Cain's two soldiers struck down the Palace Guards like bolts of lightning.

Silas watched, stunned.

The two men turned on him. He struggled and protested but he was at their mercy. They beat him and dragged him into the cell, chaining him to the wall next to Alexander. Without another word, Cain left. His two soldiers followed, Silas calling after them.

"Where are they going?" Silas asked, still trying to wrap his mind around the situation. He turned to Alexander, who had his eyes closed as if meditating.

"Alexander!" Silas snapped, fear and anger in his voice.

Without opening his eyes Alexander said, "They are taking your city."

"That's impossible!" Silas responded. "Three men cannot take a city!" But even as he spoke the words he knew the truth. Cain and his men were heading straight for the gatehouse, and once they had opened the doors there would be no stopping them.

Alexander did not respond, returning to wherever he had been before Silas interrupted.

Alexander could not tell if the muffled screaming in the distance was real or in his mind. The Seventh Legion had fallen, and the survivors were being slaughtered by their captors. Under the bodies of his friends and the fallen he crawled away, choking on the pools of blood which the saturated land had rejected. *Slowly, move slowly, only one chance.* He dragged himself, digging his elbows in and not moving his legs at all. He didn't want to attract attention. He lay still as enemy troops passed him by. They laughed and bantered like a bunch of drunken animals. One stopped, and Alexander wondered for a moment if he had been discovered. He heard the sound of the man relieving himself. Once he had finished, they continued on. Alexander looked up to see Silas among the bodies next to him. He looked tired, cold, and depressed, but not dead.

Confused, Alexander stared at him. Silas had not been at the fall of the Legion. Then Silas spoke.

"From where do you draw your strength?"

The sound of a latch brought Alexander back to himself. He sat with Silas in the dark of the prison. The temperature had dropped, and his body had begun to shiver. The door opened, and Cain returned with his men.

Silas began shouting, demanded answers, "What have you done, Cain! You have no right! We made a deal! You can't just come into this city and do as you please!"

Cain turned to leave.

Silas went silent.

"Kill them both. Outside. Let the animals feast on the dead," Cain said to his men.

"Why?" Silas demanded, groveling. "We made a deal! Besides, I am of no use to you dead!"

"I am Cain! You are a child in the den of wolves. You have no use." He left.

His men wasted no time. They unshackled the prisoners and bound their wrists with a thin twine which sliced into the skin if tampered with. They pushed the two prisoners up the stairs and out the door into the frigid morning air. Disoriented by the blinding light of the day and assaulted by the turmoil and chaos which had befallen the city, Alexander stumbled and fell. People were crying and screaming, many for the last time. Somewhere between the heat of the burning houses and the icy breath of the wind, Alexander felt death kiss him as it passed by, as if to say to him, "We will meet again soon." The winter snow was no longer pure but muddied and stained with shades of red. Whose blood it was, Alexander did not know. People screamed, and Alexander passed by bodies piled in the street. He shed a single tear. Now was not the time to weep.

They left the city by the main gate and turned north to follow along the coastal cliffs. There was a forest to the north and it was just after they had crossed into it and Omines could no longer be seen, Cain's men ordered them to stop.

"Kneel!" barked the smaller of the two men, shoving

them both forward.

Alexander dropped to his knees with a look of resignation. Silas fell to the ground, still trying to reason his way out of his mistake.

"At least have the decency to face death like a man," Alexander growled to him.

The smaller soldier took out his dagger and approached Alexander. Cain's men had made only one mistake, but it was enough. They had bound Alexander's hands in the front. The man with the dagger never would have guessed the bruised and bloodied prisoner would be so fast.

Alexander lunged forward, catching the dagger hand and forcing it back into the chest of his would-be executioner. He spun around his enemy, snatching the sword from the man's belt.

The other soldier, realizing what had happened, managed to draw his sword halfway from its scabbard before Alexander finished him.

Alexander wasted no time. He began to strip the bodies of any essential tools. He took the taller man's oversized shirt to protect himself from the cold and wind. He quickly took off the man's boots and slid his own frozen feet into them. He grabbed both swords.

"We should move," he said, cutting Silas's bonds and handing him a sword.

"You're not going to kill me?" Silas asked, confused.

"I made a promise to your father," Alexander replied.

They pressed deeper into the snow-covered forest, neither speaking for some time. Thick pines surrounded them on all sides, shielding them from the ocean wind. Silas watched the dead ice-covered brush, which seemed to be reaching up from the snow as if trying to escape the death winter had brought. Only the poison berry bushes had survived the cold, and Silas could not help but feel he was like them. Poison.

"I'm sorry," Silas began. "I betrayed you. I betrayed my kingdom. I was afraid to be a king, and after I saw you had climbed the tower, I was angry. My father wanted many things for me. I have only ever wanted her."

Alexander paused for a moment. "Your father loved you," he said.

"And I, him," Silas responded. Silence returned and they continued their aimless journey. Silas retreated back to his guilt.

"Where are we going?" Silas asked, as the woods ended just before the drop off into the ocean.

"Back," answered Alexander.

Silas stilled, as if winter's wind had frozen him straight through.

"I cannot go back," Silas stated.

"Why not? You're their King."

"I am no King. I am a coward."

"Your people need you."

"No, my people need you!" he shouted. The ferocity of the ocean seemed to match their tones, rising and falling in a great crescendo.

"What are you so afraid of?" Alexander prodded.

"I'm afraid to die!"

"You asked me where I draw my strength from?"

Silas looked puzzled. "I thought you were asleep."

"Never mind that. Did you ask?"

"Yes."

"You are not brave if you have no fear, you are a fool. True bravery is looking your fear in the face and saying, "I will never surrender." True strength is not when you overcome, but when you struggle and you grit your teeth. You decide to give something more than you thought you were capable of. You are not so much afraid to die as you are to live, Silas."

The wind caught bits of snow and sea spray, taunting

Silas as it whipped by.

"I will go. But I cannot lead them," he said.

"You must."

The sea began to pick up again.

"Do not be afraid to be their King," Alexander said, putting a hand on Silas's shoulder.

Silas gazed once more at the fallen city, his city.

"Do you have a plan?" Silas asked.

Alexander smiled and tossed Silas a berry he had picked.

"These are poisonous," Silas said.

"Exactly," Alexander answered.

In the distance, the sun set on the horizon. It melted into a potent red that seemed to permeate the land. Red, like the blood now covering the streets of the once glorious city.

The Princess had broken the rest of the mirrors and now watched through a glass prison, a canary in a cage.

Click.

There it was. The sound of the trap door latch. Cassandra turned to see the man. The man who had ascended the tower and left her with such a wonderful yet troubling message. The man who had made the climb. *Truly he was a man.*

As Cassandra looked towards the threshold of her future, she stepped away in fear. Her man had not come. Instead stood a dark figure, and he had the eyes of an animal.

Silas never thought getting back into the city would be as easy as walking in the front gate. It had been left wide open, as a mouth crying out in pain or perhaps trying to spew forth the disease which had taken it. Cain did not command kingdoms. He and his men were marauders. They came and went like the winter's wind.

After seizing the castle, Cain's men tore through the city like banshees, leaving nothing untouched. The glassy eyes of the dead reflected the firelight which consumed their beloved homes. The scent of blood and smoke hung thick in the air as black debris fell gently like snow, covering the possessions of the dead, which littered the boulevards. The path of destruction had snaked its way through the city, all the way to the palace itself.

Once the massacre had ended, the celebration had begun. The men ate, drank, and divided the spoils of war. The human remains would lie rotting until the birds picked their bones dry, a testament to the lion who had chosen his new den. As night swept across the land, those who slept now would likely sleep forever.

Silas and Alexander had scavenged enough equipment to pass as some of Cain's men.

A deep cold washed down Silas's spine as they approached the gate. His face began to feel the warmth of the fiery remains of his beloved city. The city burned as if it had been cast into hell, and the bodies of his father's people, his people, lie dead in the streets. It felt as if their ghosts had all gathered behind him and now pushed him towards the fire with their cold hands. He should burn for what he had done, he thought to himself. *I should burn forever.*

"Are you ready?" Alexander asked, looking back to him.

"Yes," Silas answered, and stepped through the gate.

Darkness had fallen across the city. Silas and Alexander used the firelight to see, sticking to the shadows. The cobblestone streets were now broken and scarred. The winter snow had melted, and blood stained each stone. Statues, monuments, and other artwork the city had treasured had been broken and tossed to the streets. Silas remained silent as they slipped through the city to the wine cellars. He would let them eat, let them drink, let them celebrate their devastating victory. Then he would strike, like a dagger: small, quick, and precise.

When they arrived at the wine cellar they found it had been picked almost clean. Only a handful of bottles remained untouched.

"This won't be enough," Alexander stated.

Silas wanted to scream. This was the only plan. It had to work. They had to make it work.

"We can water it down," Silas said, picking up two jugs. "There is a well not far from here. I will get the water. There is a cart in the back we used to use for selling the wine. Strip it and put those barrels on it. Not the big ones; the small ones. Fill them evenly with whatever wine we have left. Then we will mix the water."

Alexander smiled, but Silas didn't see it. He had left.

After several trips to the well, the barrels were almost ready. Alexander and Silas began to squeeze the poison berries, which they had brought from the wood, into each.

"Only a little in each," said Alexander, "Even if it doesn't kill them, they can't fight if they are sick as dogs."

When it was done, they put a ladle in each bucket and rolled the cart out into the street.

Alexander couldn't help but smile as Silas called out to enemy soldiers to get their wine. Out of all his time in the Legion, after all of his journeys and travels, this had to be one of the craziest things he had ever done. However, he had faith it would work.

One by one, he watched as Cain's men came over and had a few sips, then curse them for giving out such terrible drink. It had been brilliant to water down the wine. It had ensured nobody would take more than a few sips, or try to take the cart from them. They moved on, street after street, making the stops as brief as possible. The plan was not finished. They had to find the survivors and rescue them. There was no victory in saving the city if all of her people were dead. They wandered until the barrels were down to the dregs. Silas looked to Alexander, anxiety filling him.

"We will find them." Alexander said.

"I know," Silas answered.

They continued on, the city growing quieter as their work took effect. Then it grew quite loud again as Silas and Alexander came upon one of the smaller city squares. Silas remembered the local farmers had often set up their market there. People had stood in long lines waiting to get vegetables, bread, and other sorts of food. Now, there were lines of people waiting to be executed. Their tearstained faces were downcast from the knowledge of their fate. Some tried to comfort, others stood in shock. Their spirits had been broken.

Three men sat in the far corner at a table playing some sort of gambling game. Silas guessed they were higher in the ranks. Several guards walked up and down the lines, weapons drawn, keeping everyone in order as they awaited death. The executioner stood in the center with a chopping block, sharpening an incredible ax. Three more men filled a cart with the bodies of the decapitated. Silas's mouth gaped at the sight.

"Whaddya want?" grumbled an archer as he approached them. He was older and looked as though he had seen many battles. A black patch covered his left eye, and he walked with a faint limp.

Everyone turned to the newcomers.

"We have more wine!" Silas exclaimed, trying to sound excited and perhaps a bit tipsy.

The archer looked into the buckets and cocked his

head a bit.

"Doesn't seem like ya got much left," he stated.

Silas wanted to kick himself for not dumping the remnants in to just one or two buckets to make it seem as though they had more.

"Bring it here anyway!" shouted one of the men at the gambling table, who stood and waved.

Silas smiled and nodded at the archer as he and Alexander pushed the cart towards the table.

"Wait!" came a cry, distant at first but it grew louder.

Silas turned to see a man running up to the archer. He recognized him. Alexander had served some of his friends wine but this man hadn't drunk any. Silas glanced at Alexander, who remembered as well. Their hoax was done. Silas exploded towards the two men, drawing his sword and slashing off the messenger's head. Spinning with a practiced grace, he drove the blade through the archer, before anyone knew what was happening. Silas let the blade fall with the old man, grabbing his bow as he went. The first arrow was nocked and ready as the first of his opponents charged him. He released the arrow and it struck true.

Alexander charged the three men at the table and made quick work of them. He turned with just enough time to dodge the ax blade of the executioner. A small battle ensued, ending with the people of Omines looking to their saviors.

Silas stood before them, Alexander at his side.

"Let us take back our home!" the Prince shouted.

Using whatever they could find as weapons, the last men of Omines went to work reclaiming their city. The streets, once a testament to the glory of man, now black and charred, seemed to be a tribute to death. As the survivors passed through the streets, many could not help but feel that they were in some foreign place. Had they not known what had wrought such destruction they might have guessed a dragon had attacked. They kept to the shadows, following the sounds of laughter, cutting the throats of the drunk and unsuspecting invaders as they went. As they reached the center of the city, they came upon a mob of men feasting outside of the palace. The moment had come: this would decide the fate of their city. Together the men of Omines stepped out into the light and descended upon the enemy, tearing them to pieces.

"Silas," Alexander called. "It's time!"

Silas knew what he meant, and together they left the fray to find Cain.

The enemy had soiled their beloved city, and the throne room was no exception. The six pillars which led to the throne were the only things still intact. The walls, once beautiful with mosaics, were now broken, shards of stone littering the floor. A fire burned bright in the center pit.

Cain sat upon the throne. Scars covered his defined body, and he looked like a sculpture of a war god. Everything about him seemed to worship death, except the spark of life that passed through his eyes.

By his side, Alexander saw the girl from the tower. She stood next to the throne, bound by a slave's chains, one on each wrist and another at her throat. Even in captivity, her beauty shone through. Her eyes held an ocean of sorrow within them and a desire to be free of it all. As she watched Alexander approach, her eyes seemed to change and hold a drop of hope.

"Cain!" Alexander called, "This is between us!"

Cain rose from the throne, pulling the girl closer with one arm, raising her to her tiptoes by her chains. She wiggled and writhed as her bonds began to choke her. A twisted smile passed across Cain's lips, as if he were a demented child who was enjoying torturing his new puppy.

"Let her go!" Alexander commanded.

"Women," Cain said, lowering her just enough for her to gasp. "I will never understand the fascination." He licked the side of her face.

Alexander bore down on Cain with a fury like never before. Cain shoved the girl to the floor, reaching for his weapon. Alexander's sword came crashing down as Cain's rose to meet it.

Silas froze, watching the spectacle; two gods locked in combat, equal in skill and determination. He tried to rush to his friend's aid but Cain saw him coming. Shifting his weight, Cain sent Alexander sprawling into Silas's path. The two collided and toppled to the floor. Cain didn't miss a beat. Everything happened so fast Silas hardly noticed the burning sensation run through his arm as he scrambled to his feet. He watched as Cain's blade continued past him, a trail of blood reaching through the air after the cold steel. Silas toppled away as Alexander shoved him out of the path of the next blow. Catching Alexander off-balance, Cain disarmed him in an instant. Then with his free hand he grabbed Alexander and heaved him across the throne room.

Alexander sprang to his feet, but the shark had gotten his first scent of blood. Cain crossed the room to Silas and, after a brief skirmish, disarmed him as well. Alexander knew most of the atrocities which had gained Cain the name of savage, but he was still surprised when Cain tackled Silas, howling like an animal, and began to beat, bite, and claw him. Silas covered his head with his arms, protecting himself as much as he could as Cain tried to tear him apart.

Alexander grabbed Cain from behind, in a chokehold. Cain slipped free, and Alexander retrieved his sword. They stood face to face once more. Alexander began the dance again, and this time death danced with them.

"No!" Cassandra cried, and the world seemed to freeze in answer.

Silas watched the iron clasps bite into her outstretched arms as Cassandra reached for Alexander. It was too late. Cain's blade slipped into Alexander's midsection and out the other side. Then, with a quick jerking motion, Cain pulled his sword back out.

Alexander dropped to a knee, a look of disbelief flashing across his face. Then Cain grabbed him by his armor and dragged the fallen soldier across the throne room. Alexander trailed behind him like a rag doll, choking on the blood dribbling out of his mouth.

Silas sprang up, his destiny clear. He had tried to run from it, but now he would honor the memory of his father or join him in the afterlife. He ran towards the balcony after them, grabbing Alexander's fallen sword as he went.

Cain turned to face him.

Clang after clang sounded as the two swords met and Silas matched Cain. And with each passing moment his fear faded.

Snow had begun to fall from the cloud-covered night sky, and the waves of the ocean crashed below. With a final savage strike, Cain shattered Silas' sword and watched as a look of realization passed over the young Prince's face. He would die tonight. He turned away, desperately looking for something with which to defend himself. His eyes caught on the girl sobbing in chains. *Who is she?* he wondered. Then, realizing how absurd the thought was, he turned back to face his enemy. But Cain was gone. One moment Silas had stood face to face with death and the next, he stood alone. He looked over the edge of the balcony and found Cain gripping the banister, muscles bulging as he tried to pull himself back up.

Alexander had mustered his strength and, grabbing

Cain from behind, had thrown himself backward over the terrace edge. Even now, face white as a ghost, Alexander still held on. He was a dead man haunting his killer.

Silas met Alexander's eyes. No words were spoken, and none were necessary. Alexander slipped one of the daggers out of Cain's belt and stabbed Cain through the back of the heart.

Silas watched as death embraced them both and dragged them to the depths of the ocean.

Omines was reclaimed that night, and Cain's army was defeated. The city mourned for weeks but rebuilt itself. Silas was crowned King. A monument was built in honor of the great hero Alexander. It was not until later that Cassandra realized her hands were still scraped and face was still bruised. The curse had been broken. She and Silas spent much time together, and she never spoke of her origins.

One night she found Silas burning his paintings.

"Who is she?" Cassandra asked.

"There is a legend, here in Omines, of a princess locked in the tower," Silas began

"I know the legend," she interrupted.

"These are her." He continued, "or at least my perception of her."

Silas watched as the fire did its work.

"Did you love her?" Cassandra asked.

"I thought I did," Silas answered, "but the truth is I fell in love with an illusion. All of these paintings, all of my thoughts. They were beautiful, but not real."

His thoughts fell to a story he had heard once, though he could not remember from where. It was the story of a painter. He shuddered at the thought.

"Sometimes fate has something better for us than what

we think we want," he concluded. He turned, leaving his art to burn, and walked to Cassandra. He smoothed back her hair from her face. Even with the scars Cain had left on her she was beautiful. In his eyes, she always would be.

"I love you, Cassandra."

"I love you, too."

He kissed her gently on the lips. Then together they watched his art burn.

"What do you think will happen to her?" he asked. "The girl in the tower."

"I think she will be fine."

THE WOLF

4

A crack in the clouds permitted the full moon to peek through for a moment, as if it were the eye of some god who wished to spy upon his creation. Then it passed, and the prisoner found himself once more shrouded in darkness. Sweat-soaked locks of hair hung around his bowed face, shielding him, like the hands of a man hiding his face in shame. Torches burned above him like a funeral pyre, and he felt as though he were in a grave rather than a prison cell. This spot had been reserved for the most dangerous of criminals. It was a twelve-foot deep hole in the edge of a mountain, with a steel grate over the top to seal it. Prison guards murmured to each other, keeping their distance from the hole. A sense of uneasiness blanketed the mountainside.

An uncomfortable iron collar had been clamped around his neck and linked to each wrist by chains. An observer might have mistaken him for a praying man. The prisoner knelt as though imploring a god who either wasn't listening or simply wasn't there. Pain. Pain had been his companion through the years, not god. It had been there before he had damned himself, and the prisoner was quite certain pain would follow him should there be an afterlife. He would have spent his whole life in prison if he thought it could free him from pain. That had become his only desire: to be free of the pain, even if only for a few moments.

For a second time the moon peaked down at the earth

through the clouds. The prisoner looked up, unfazed. The light was no more dangerous than the dark. Darkness cannot create monsters, just as light does not destroy them. It is in darkness that monsters hide and in light that they are revealed. From deep in his throat came a fierce sound: not the roar of an animal, but the cry of a man who has lost everything. Then, shuddering, he surrendered once more, shedding his humanity like a snakeskin.

The coolness of the river's water felt good on Daniel's skin as he submerged himself in it. The sensation shocked him a little, but he knew it was not so much the temperature of the water but rather the contrast to the hot, thick summer air which hung over the breezeless land. As Daniel held his breath under the surface, he began to count in his mind. The gentle touch of the flowing liquid seemed to relinquish its embrace, letting its icy hands slip away. The slow current massaged him. He felt soothed and revitalized, as if he had just stepped out of the world and all of its chaos. He had left his problems on the shoreline. Here, in the weightlessness, there was peace. Here, in the gentle hum of the stream, he felt safe.

"Get out!" he heard someone cry.

Daniel couldn't tell if someone had called to him or if it had been a trick of his imagination as he broke the tension of the water's surface. He stood in the center of the river, looking to his left at the rock embankment. The river cut through a great forest; and though Daniel would not have been able to point to his position on a map, he was quite sure he was too deep in the forest to be close to any people. He began to walk towards the boulder where he had left his sword and satchel, his only possessions other than his garments, which had also needed a good cleaning and still hung on his body. He searched the tree line with a careful eye as he went. Daniel froze in disbelief as his eyes fell upon a distant bloodstained figure, her eyes seeming to call to him from across eternity.

"Get out!" he heard again.

He remained motionless. The subtle hum of the river seemed to have hypnotized him, swaying him back and forth, in accord with its will. And now her ghost stood before him, casting yet another spell over him. He would drown himself in the river should she only speak the command.

The sound of a dog barking broke the enchantment. Daniel looked back towards the rock where he had left his sword to see a shaggy gray haired dog and a frantic young boy waving his hands.

"Please, mister! Get out of the water!" the boy implored.

Daniel's gaze returned to where the woman had stood, but she was gone. He began to wade towards the boy and the dog when a third figure appeared, a man who looked to be the boy's father.

"Isaac! Isaac, get back!" he snapped, brandishing a long sturdy walking stick.

"We have to warn him," the boy pleaded.

Daniel didn't quite catch the response. The man whispered to his son; after a moment, the son's face turned to one of fear, and he cowered behind his father.

"Stop right there, stranger!" the man shouted to Daniel as Daniel walked unfazed over the rock shore. "Show me your neck!"

Daniel understood, and with slow deliberate motions he removed his shirt, revealing the countless white scars which marbled his well-defined body. He tilted his head to either side to show the lack of a werewolf bite.

"I mean you no harm," he said, raising his hands.

The father's demeanor changed.

"I'm sorry. We believe there is a werewolf in these parts."

"How's that?"

"Follow the river upstream about a day's walk and you will find a prison. Something got out of it. Left no survivors. It looked-"

The man paused, glancing towards his son, then back to Daniel.

"Like the work of a beast," he finished.

Daniel nodded.

"My name's Joshua. This is my son, Isaac," the man said, extending his hand.

"Hi," Isaac said, creeping out from his father's shadow.

Daniel smiled at the boy and stepped forward to take the father's hand when he heard a low growl.

"Easy, Roland," Joshua said. "He thinks he's a hunting dog. He's lucky if he can find his own way back home."

The dog backed away at his master's voice without taking its eyes off Daniel, leaving the impression it did not like him.

"My name is Daniel," Daniel said, as the two men shook hands.

"My son wasn't wrong to want to warn you," Joshua said. "That werewolf is around these parts somewhere. You have the look of a traveling man. You have a place to stay?"

Daniel wasn't sure how to take the comment but figured Joshua probably knew most of the people in the area, and didn't mean it as an insult.

"No, sir, I can't say I do. Is there a town around here you could point me towards?"

"About a full day's walk in that direction," Joshua said with a pointed finger. "But it's almost dinnertime, after which it will be too dark to travel. Why don't you come with us? We have a small pig farm just back behind the tree line."

"I don't want to be a burden," Daniel stated.

"Nonsense!" Joshua smiled. "Give me a hand with the

farm chores tomorrow, and we will call it even."

"Does this mean I don't have chores tomorrow?" Isaac asked, excitement in his voice.

"Don't be silly; of course you do," Joshua smiled, turning his attention back to Daniel. "Do you have any things you need to collect?"

Daniel was impressed with the man's generosity. He hadn't even waited for Daniel to accept the invitation.

"Not much," Daniel said, walking to the boulder and retrieving his things.

"Woah!" Isaac exclaimed, seeing the sword.

As Daniel came closer, Joshua noticed the hilt, a howling wolf made of steel.

"Well, I'll be." Joshua shook his head in disbelief. "You're the hunter."

"Who is he?" Isaac asked, confused.

"A legend," his father answered.

The last rays of light that had managed to penetrate the thick canopy of the forest had almost dissipated. A steady growing wind had begun to move through the trees, ushering some far off storm closer. Joshua proved good at making small talk, and Daniel was appreciative, having walked in silence enough on his own. He was not afraid to be alone with his thoughts, but he did not relish the idea either. They walked through the woods before coming upon a path that cut through the forest. Isaac and the dog ran ahead but always stayed within sight of Joshua. Daniel wondered what adventures the boy must be having in his mind, as he watched Isaac swing a small branch he had picked up in a way which was unmistakably a sword. He missed those days. As boys, battles are waged in the realm of imagination; as men, wars rage within the mind, but they are not imaginary and there is no victor.

The tree line broke on one side of the path, opening up to a small valley of tall grass with a little pig farm in its center. A small cabin had been erected from logs in the center. The trees had been cut, stripped, and stacked, then cut again with notches close to the edges to create intersecting slots for support. Many of the townhouses in the areas surrounding the forest were made with the same design. Joshua explained to Daniel how the small overhang above the front doorway served a double purpose. It provided more room in the loft where the family slept, and it also served as a sort of canopy when it rained. A small chimney protruded from the roof, through which wafted little puffs of smoke. Daniel judged by the smoke that there was a small fire that, due to the intense heat of the day, would only be used for cooking. He wiped his brow subconsciously.

Coming to the edge of the tall grass, Daniel saw how it had been cleared away around the house, making way for hard dry dirt caked with bits of hay. A wooden fence branched off to the left, creating a sty for about thirty pigs. A small shelter had been set up for them, and a trough ran half the length of one of the fences.

A small fire pit and a well completed their small safe haven, tucked away and hidden from the world. Several windows had their shutters, open and Daniel could hear the sound of pots, pans, and laughter inside. The scent of a warm stew reached him before he was anywhere near the door. Daniel looked down at Roland to see the dog had begun salivating too.

As they entered the house, Daniel felt as though he had been dropped into a furnace. Even with all of the shutters open, the breezeless summer air hung thick and heavy. To his right stood a woman putting the finishing touches on the dinner she had prepared.

Isaac pushed by him in a hurry and scampered around

the large table to join his sisters in a tiny corner of the house. One was still a child of three or four, and the other, a young woman of nineteen or perhaps twenty. The elder sister stood upon a wooden crate that had been set as a makeshift sort of stage. The sound of her smooth voice enchanted her two siblings and also Daniel. Dark brown locks swayed in loose waves just shy of her shoulders, like stage curtains out from which she would peer. Her deep green eyes overflowed with passion and drama, and for a moment they gazed intently upon him.

"Daniel," Joshua said, placing a hand on his shoulder.

Daniel turned.

"I'd like you to meet my wife, Nora."

The woman who had been finishing the preparations now stood before him, offering him a warm smile.

"This is Daniel," Joshua continued.

"It's a pleasure to have you with us tonight," she stated.

Daniel noted that her accent was from a neighboring land he had once visited. It was not far, but her accent still surprised him. Most did not move this far out into the country.

"It's an honor to be here," he replied, answering in her native language.

"Well now," she said in a playful tone, turning to her husband. "Where did you find him? Did you and the boy somehow manage to get to the city and back today? Hmmm."

"I am just a traveler, familiar with many cities and many tongues." Daniel continued, switching back.

"And what brings you out to these parts?" Nora asked. "It's become quite dangerous of late."

Daniel could not manage to suppress a wry smile.

"What, have you not warned him?" Nora asked, turning to her husband.

Joshua motioned for Daniel to show her his sword and Daniel unstrapped the sheath which held his sword across his shoulders. He cradled it in his arms, holding it out to Nora hilt first, exposing the image crafted on its handle.

Nora cupped her hands over her mouth, speechless. Joshua leaned in close to her, whispering just loud enough for Daniel to hear. "Imagine my surprise when I did."

"Are you here to save us?" she asked.

Daniel opened his mouth to answer, not sure of what would have come out had he had time to answer. The elder daughter saved him by calling from the other side of the room.

"Is dinner ready, mother? I'm not sure I can entertain them much longer."

Daniel looked over to see Isaac had begun to antagonize his baby sister, poking her.

Nora excused herself to put supper on the table. Joshua called to the children and introduced them one by one. The little girl's name was Bella. The eldest daughter was Susan. Due to the age gap, Daniel wondered if there had been other children but dared not ask.

They all sat down, Joshua at one head of the table, Daniel at the other. Joshua raised his hands and bowed his head for a blessing. The rest of the family did the same, taking hands and bowing their heads. Daniel was familiar with the custom and took the hands of Isaac on his left and Susan on his right. Her smooth skin reminded him of the statues of the goddesses he had seen in ancient cities. She flinched at his touch.

"Dear Lord," Joshua began. "We thank you for these gifts you have provided for us. We praise you. Bless all the nations of the world. And all less fortunate than us. Keep us safe from harm."

"Now and forever," they all responded.

Daniel looked up to see Susan's eyes dart away.

"You're a believer," Nora said, half statement, half question.

Throughout the region, there were only two religious groups: the followers and the believers.

Altars and shrines had been scattered throughout the country, but no one quite knew who had built them. With no history of origin, it was believed they had existed since the creation of the world.

Altars were dedicated to Nos, an evil spirit. His worshippers were known as followers. When travelers passed an altar, legend said, they must spill blood upon it to avoid the curse of Nos. It could be a tiny cut on the hand, but the blood must be smeared on the altar. Once a year, followers were required to gather and offer human sacrifice. Worship of Nos had been outlawed in many cities, but there were still a fair number who practiced it, most of whom were werewolves.

The shrines, however, had been built to a nameless benevolent God. His worshippers were known as believers. Though some people moved out to the shrines and became hermits, most offered a simple prayer when passing and small thanksgivings before meals.

"I am familiar with the customs," Daniel replied. "And I was raised to believe."

"But you don't any longer?" Joshua asked. His voice was not condescending but held genuine curiosity.

Daniel looked to the younger children, conscious his answer could raise more questions.

"I've just seen a little too much."

Joshua nodded, chewing his food, understanding. What Daniel had meant was *I have seen too much evil.*

"It's funny; I would think that would have deepened your faith," Nora replied.

Daniel contemplated her words. There cannot be shadows without light. Evil in some twisted sense proves the existence of good. However, Daniel's answer had been a simple one. It had not only been the things he had *seen* which had pushed him from the faith.

"Can we have a fire tonight, dad?" Isaac asked, changing the subject.

Joshua looked to his wife. "It would be fun. It would be a good way to keep away any unwanted company."

"Like a werewolf!" Isaac shouted.

Joshua winced.

Bella's eyes widened with fear, and she began to cry. Joshua took the child, cradling her in his arms and began making the "shhh" sound, which is only comforting to a child when they are in their parent's arms. His eyes darted over to Isaac, reminding him to watch his words in front of his little sister.

They finished dinner, speaking of the night's later festivities, singing and stories by a fire. Susan did not look at Daniel again.

After dinner, Joshua and Isaac ran around the pigsty together, lighting the torches which had been tethered to each of the fence posts. It was a tradition the men of the family performed every time there was a wolf sighting close by, Nora explained, as Daniel lit his pipe and began to prepare a bonfire.

"Are you sure this is wise?" Daniel asked. "Fire has been known to scare away wolves, but I have fought some who have seen it as a challenge."

She shrugged. "There is not much else we can do. My husband and I believe that the light will keep away the creatures of the dark."

"I hope you know I meant no disrespect, ma'am," Daniel stated.

"Not to worry. When I believe you have disrespected me, you will know," she said with a smile before leaving him to his work. Roland sauntered over to him as she left. He watched with stoic eyes as Daniel continued preparing the fire. He reached out to the dog but Roland simply turned his head as if he hadn't noticed. His tongue hung out lazily as he panted in the night's heat. Daniel could not help but feel the dog believed he was either Daniel's guardian or slave master.

Once the fire was burning, they all sat close as the night had begun to cool. Daniel watched as the darkness began to circle around them, like a silent animal stalking its prey, creeping closer and closer until the fire-light became too much. He sat with his sword close by. They sang songs, and Joshua played an old guitar. Though Daniel was not a confident singer he joined in the songs he knew. As the night grew later, Nora and Joshua went in to put Bella to bed, leaving their other two children in the care of the wolf slayer and their dog, Roland.

Daniel loaded his pipe with tobacco. Isaac watched with interest at first but soon began to toy with his father's guitar.

"Stop it, Isaac; you know better," Susan demanded.

The boy persisted before she snatched it away.

"You will wake up Bella!" she reminded him.

Isaac sulked before a new idea came to him.

"Tell a story!" he exclaimed.

"No."

"Please!" Isaac whined. "You tell the best ones. She does the voices and everything!"

"Isaac!" Susan said, flushing under the gaze of their guest.

Isaac shot her a look which would have melted his mother's heart, had she not been putting Bella to bed.

"Alright," Susan gave in. "But no voices tonight," she continued, brushing a loose strand of hair behind her ear. It was strange, but in that simple motion, it was as if the young woman had opened a vial of perfume into the air. A scent so faint but so sweet. Then it was gone.

"There was once a hunter who traveled the world fighting evil. He was brave, strong, and rather dashing in an odd way." She began looking from Isaac to Daniel, catching his eyes.

"No matter what stood against him he would always win, because he was pure of heart. One day he came upon a small village as they prepared to sacrifice a beautiful maiden. He demanded to know the reason, and he was told the town had been plagued by werewolves."

As she spoke she had inched herself towards her little brother and at the mention of werewolves she held her hands high up over her head, making pretend claws and growling. Her movement was so quick it looked as if she lunged. Isaac jumped, startled, an expression of fear covering his face. Susan began to laugh.

"That's not funny," Isaac whined, looking away.

Quite satisfied with herself, Susan ignored his comment and continued her story.

"The men had hoped to appease the werewolves by leaving the poor girl for their amusement. When the man heard of this, he swore he would hunt all of the wolves down and kill them. One by one he tricked all of the wolves, waiting in a field dressed as a sheep. When the wolves attacked he would kill them with his sword. But the last one had been the leader and was smarter than the rest."

Daniel watched, amused, as the fire grew bigger in the reflection of Isaac's wide eyes. The young boy's mouth gaped open as he listened, imagining an epic battle of one man fighting off half a dozen werewolves.

"The werewolf came into the village and kidnapped the beautiful maiden the hunter had been trying so hard to save. So the hunter skinned one of the dead wolves and, wearing its hide as if it were his own skin, went to the leader's den, pretending to be a fellow werewolf. The leader was not expecting this and let the hunter in. Then the hunter killed him.

"Then he rescued the maiden. To show her appreciation, she made him a special sword, as she was the daughter of the village blacksmith. It had a symbol on the hilt so all wolves would know to be wary of him. Then the maiden and the hunter fell in love and got married, and they lived happily for many years," Susan ended.

"Ever after," Isaac said.

"What?" Susan asked, confused.

"They lived happily ever after," Isaac repeated. "That's how all the stories end."

Shocked by Isaac's statement, Susan glanced at Daniel.

"Right, Daniel?" Isaac asked.

How Susan knew so much of his story, Daniel did not know, but he knew how *this* story had to end.

"I believe your brother is right," he said, looking at Susan, then to Isaac. "They lived happily ever after," Daniel repeated.

"I think it's time for bed," Joshua said to his children, returning to the fire.

"Oh, dad, you missed it!" Isaac said, running up to his father and retelling the tale. He missed a few parts and embellished a great deal on the battles; but Daniel didn't notice as he looked at the young woman before him. She gave a halfhearted smile and nodded as if to say, "Thank you." It reminded him of the look a scolded child makes when offering an apology. He returned the subtle nod. She rose, excusing herself, but he stopped her, catching her hand gently.

"Where did you hear that story, miss?" he asked. "If you don't mind."

"A boy from town told it to me," she said, flushing.

He nodded again, satisfied with her answer.

The fire had begun to burn low, and they all retired to

the house. Joshua showed Daniel a corner of the house they kept available for visitors. He provided several blankets and a rice sack for Daniel to use as a pillow. Daniel thanked his host and assured him the fire would be extinguished before Daniel returned to sleep. Then he went back to the smoldering fire with his pipe and fell into his thoughts, the quiet popping of the wood not disturbing him in the slightest.

The beast circled the small farmhouse as silent as a serpent slithering through the shallows. A scent had caught its nose... had it been sheep or goats the beast might have ignored it; but this smell had been the smell of perfume, and like a shark to blood, the werewolf had come to this quiet little farm. Unnoticed, it snuck into the pen, where the pigs gave a light squeal sensing a predator. The wolf had tried to avoid the farm altogether, but under the influence of the smell it had given in and, though it had not discovered the source of the scent, it had found pigs. It eyed each of them from the shadows, mouth watering and body shaking, ready for the kill. Then out of the silence came the low sound of a growl. The beast looked over to see a small dog emerge from the doorway of the house. The wolf exposed his fangs, less like a predator and more like a clown smiling, as the dog raised his nose to the air, trying to catch the scent of the intruder. As it lowered its snout to the ground to follow the trail, the beast lunged from the shadow and killed the dog where it stood.

Daniel awoke in the middle of the night with the sense something was wrong. Wiping the film from his eyes, he looked to see blood on the floor. He froze, wide awake...Or was he? He stepped cautiously across the wooden slats of the floor, following the deep crimson trail which led to the outside of the small farmhouse where he had taken up residence. He reached for his sword as he made his way to the door, drawing it from its sheath as he crossed the threshold. He brushed the door aside as he passed through and into the night. As the door opened and revealed the trail of blood that continued on to the pig's pen, Daniel's heart fell. And then he saw her: his wife, lying on the ground beside the pen's rail, eyes and mouth wide open as if crying out to a god that had abandoned her in her time of need. Her light blue robes, which Daniel had purchased for her, were stained in the deep crimson residue of life. He ran to her and dropped to his knees. Scooping her up in his arms, he felt the gentle brush of fur against his face. He opened his eyes to the sight of Roland, who had died for the family he served. Daniel held the poor dog close, having no questions in his mind as to the dog's end, and wept softly into the night.

In the morning Daniel explained to Joshua how several of the pigs were missing and how the valiant dog had met its end. They wasted no time in laying Roland to rest, burying him on the edge of their land. Isaac and Bella cried, as Susan averted her face. Joshua held his children, trying to console them. Daniel looked into the distance, ever watchful of the tree line. After a while Nora scooped up the exhausted Bella in her arms and, taking Isaac by the hand, led them back to their home.

"Time to go," Joshua stated.

"I'd like to stay here awhile, if it's alright," Susan whispered.

Joshua opened his mouth as if to speak, then released a deep sigh.

"I'll stay with her," Daniel offered, placing a hand on Joshua's shoulder.

Joshua nodded and left in silence. Daniel knew there were few things in the world worse than watching someone you loved in pain. Although Joshua would miss the dog, he was more distraught by the pain that had been brought to his family.

Daniel stood back far enough to respect her privacy. The wind had picked up and tossed her hair as though some frantic ghost clawed at her, afraid to be swept away. Her small frame had begun to tremble, whether from the cold or tears Daniel did not know. He removed his cloak.

"Here, miss," he said, wrapping it around her. "There's no sense in you joining him."

"If there is a god, why does he allow this?" She spoke so softly he barely heard it.

"Death?" Daniel asked.

"Pain," Susan corrected.

Daniel nodded. He had traveled many lands and seen his fair share of pain. He began to wonder about her answer. *Pain.* Did she mean the pain of losing a pet? Or was there more?

"Either he is a cruel god or there is a reason for it," he offered.

"Or?" she prompted.

Daniel sighed, turning his head to look back at the farmhouse. The others had gone inside.

"Or god is a fairy tale invented by people to ease the terror of how meaningless the world is," he said, his gaze returning to the young woman.

"Do you pray?" she asked, knowing his answer from dinner the previous night.

"Not anymore."

She turned to him, brushing her tears away as she did so.

"Why not?" she asked, staring at him. Since the moment he had met her, her eyes had teased him. The deep green seemed to hold not just the light but some sort of mystery. It was as if her thoughts had been written in them and then blurred, just enough to leave a vague impression of what they had been. A clue, a shape, and just when you thought you could read it you realized it made no sense. It was just a handful of scattered words.

But this look was different. It was a stare he feared could see straight into his soul. Not a gaze of intimacy, but rather intensity. What if, through some strange divination, she could see down into his very personhood and everything about him lay bare before her? What if she did know his whole story, not just pieces? His wife stood before him, garments saturated in blood, staring at him with the same deep, glassy, green-gray eyes. Fear crept into his mind. Then Susan turned away. *No,* he thought. She had seen nothing. He was being foolish.

Daniel didn't answer.

"I've stopped praying," she continued. "I am afraid if I cry out to God he will answer, letting me know his will is not like mine and he is the root of pain, or I will call out and hear nothing but the wind and the silence."

Daniel remained quiet.

"I want to leave," she said.

"We can go back," he said, resting his hands on her shoulders in a paternal fashion.

"No," she exclaimed, shrugging away and whipping around towards him. "I want to leave *here!*"

The wind caught her words but also caught her scent.

Lovely was too simple a word for it. It was a complex fragrance which reminded Daniel of some long forgotten memory. It was earthy yet sweet, like a field of fresh strawberries after the summer rain.

It caught him so off-guard he almost did not respond. Then he realized what she had said and more so what she had meant. She wished to leave her home.

"You think that you will be safer from pain out there?" he scoffed, pointing into the woods.

"No…" she said, her face falling. "All I know is I don't want to wait here for my death. We live in pain, we die in pain. I just don't want to live and die here like Roland."

You don't have to leave to escape your pain, Daniel thought, but he remained silent. He reached into his pocket for his pipe before remembering he had left it in the house. He cursed under his breath. Their conversation was over. Her eyes again became a great mystery. They walked back to the farm in silence, the wind calling and the tall grass reaching after them.

From the moment Daniel met Thomas he didn't like him.

After Daniel and Susan had left poor Roland's grave they had returned to the house to find Daniel was no longer the only visitor. The neighbor, a young man named Thomas, had come to visit. He had rushed out to greet them, and Daniel, sensing danger, had almost drawn his sword and killed Thomas on the spot. Now, as they all sat around the table, Daniel almost wished he had. It was not because he had been rude to Daniel. The awkward boy had stopped a few feet in front of Susan as if waiting for permission to embrace her. Susan, trying to be polite, side-stepped this by introducing Thomas to Daniel. Thomas had barely acknowledged him, making it clear he was not looking for any more friends. But Daniel's distaste for Thomas stemmed from something else: something just beneath the surface, underneath the sweet façade Thomas had put on for the dinner table. Whatever it was it still eluded Daniel. It was like entering a tavern and smelling food, but not being able to tell what the food was. The scent was only enough to tease the memory but not summon it.

Daniel watched Thomas drape his arm over the back of Susan's chair, leaning in to whisper something to her. He was older than Susan, with a medium build, light brown hair, and brown eyes; and he glanced at Daniel as he pulled back, leaving his arm as it lay. Susan glanced at Daniel, a spark lit within those deep mysterious eyes. She ate her soup so casually and disinterestedly, he couldn't help but feel she knew Thomas was trying to lay claim to her. More than that, she wasn't stopping him. She was waiting to see what Daniel would do. She was playing the two men off of each other, and he would be lying if he said it wasn't working in the slightest.

"Has your father been having any trouble with his sheep?" Joshua asked, as Nora served the stew she had prepared for dinner.

"No," Thomas answered, oblivious to what Joshua meant.

"He hasn't heard any rumors about a wild dog in the area?" Joshua tried again, not wanting to upset Bella, who seemed more intent on the soup her mother was serving than their conversation. But you could never be sure with children.

"Oh you mean…" Thomas began, before Joshua shot a glance to his youngest child, and Thomas understood. He gave a slow nod. "Yes, he has heard about it. But no one has seen it."

"Maybe the werewolf got it!" Isaac said. "Dad thinks there's one of those too."

Sure enough, as soon as Isaac said it, Bella's face changed as if snapped out of a dream; and no longer interested in her mother's cooking, she began to cry.

"I no wanna be eated!" she exclaimed.

Joshua looked to his son with an expression only a parent can give.

"Don't cry, Bella." Daniel said, "If a big old wolf comes, I won't let him eat you. I'll send him home to his mama."

Isaac giggled at the statement, and Bella ran to Daniel, crawling up onto his lap and hiding her face in his chest.

"Pwomise?" she asked.

"That's right," Daniel said, cradling her. "I promise."

"You think you could fight a werewolf?" Thomas asked with a chuckle. Susan burst into laughter, and Thomas stared at her for a moment before asking her what was so funny.

"Remember the story you told me? About the wolf hunter?" she asked, still giggling. "Last summer?"

"Yes," Thomas replied, still confused.

"Daniel *is* the hunter."

The look in Thomas's eyes flashed from disbelief to fear. It lasted only for a moment, but it was all Daniel had needed. He had seen beneath the mask even if only for a second. There had been a new scent when he and Susan had returned earlier. One so subtle he hadn't even noticed it. But now it was clear as day. Even through the potent aroma of the soup Daniel could smell the wolf. It was not a strong smell, which meant Thomas was a young wolf; or perhaps he had merely been around them. Either way, it was clear he had been meddling in things far beyond him.

After dinner Joshua put Isaac and Bella to bed, as the events of the day had drained them. Thomas asked Susan to join him outside to watch the last of the sunset, and Daniel offered to help Nora clean up from dinner. She cleared everything and swept while he went out to fetch a bucket of water. When he returned he set it on the counter and began to wash the small wooden plates and other utensils, watching Thomas through the open window. He had taken Susan by the hand and walked her to the far edge of the field where the tree line opened just enough to see the sunset.

It was not long before Nora joined Daniel, grabbing a rag to dry his work. She had the slightest twinkle in her eye, and Daniel found himself worried for the second time that one of the women of this family was seeing more of him than he had wished.

"Is your wife's passing what caused you to lose your faith?" she asked in the gentlest tone she could conjure.

"Susan told you?" Daniel asked.

"She told me nothing. But just as you know my first language, my city knows the story of the great wolf hunter. You travel alone, with no family and no faith, only a deep sorrow in your eyes."

"My wife was murdered by the beast," he answered. "I have done many things but none as terrible as bringing my dead wife before the shrine of a god with no name."

Nora watched Daniel, his eyes darkened with emotion. She reached out to him, putting a hand on his shoulder in a way which reminded Daniel of his own mother. "I am sorry for your loss, Daniel."

"It was not your fault," he replied, looking back to his work only to find he had finished. "Do you ever wonder," he asked. "If maybe he gave us no name to cry out in our time of need because, if he is real, he wants nothing to do with us?"

"No," she answered. Then after a moment's thought, she asked, "Why do you believe he wants nothing to do with you?"

"I'd rather not call attention to my bad habits. If you haven't caught them yet, maybe I'm not as far gone as I thought," he answered, dodging the question. He had meant it to sound like a joke, but he wasn't sure it had.

"I think you're too hard on yourself," Nora answered, putting the last of the bowls in the cupboard. "My only gripe is you smoke too much," she said, as Daniel produced his pipe from his shirt. She winked at him. "I never much cared for the smell."

"If it were only that," Daniel whispered.

A brief moment passed before Daniel changed the subject. "What is the boy's story?"

Nora sighed and smiled. "He is a young man from

town a few miles away. He comes from a good family, and he stops by every few days to see our daughter. He is persistent." They both walked over to the doorway, peering out towards the setting sun. It had sunk low like the eyelids of a child who was about to surrender to sleep. The air was becoming cool but not cold. And in the distance, on the crest of the hill overlooking the farm, the silhouette of two figures could be seen.

Daniel didn't need to ask to know Susan did not reciprocate the boy's feelings.

"Perhaps I should go rescue her?" he mused, chewing on the end of his pipe.

Nora smiled again. "Perhaps you should."

Daniel lit his pipe and set out across the field to retrieve the two. As he approached Susan and Thomas, he deliberately made more noise than necessary so as not to startle them. Susan turned to face him. Thomas either didn't care or pretended not to hear.

"Daniel, come sit with us." Susan beckoned, moving over and creating a space between her and Thomas.

"I'm afraid I cannot," he replied. "Your mother wants you back inside; it's almost dark."

Susan rose and brushed off her dress.

"Let me walk you back," Thomas offered, extending his hand.

"The house is just over there," Susan countered. "I'm sure I can make it."

Thomas was about to say something else before Daniel interrupted.

"I was hoping to have a word with you," he said, gesturing to Thomas with his pipe. The young man's gaze shifted from Daniel to Susan, then back to Daniel again.

140

"Of course," he muttered.

Susan gave a polite nod to Daniel before she turned to leave. The two men stood watching her until she entered through the doorway of her house. A soft amber glow of tobacco illuminated Daniel's face as he turned to Thomas.

"I know what you are," he said.

"And I you," Thomas replied, not bothering to face him.

"I will give you one warning. Stay away from this family. As long as you are a wolf, you have no business here."

Thomas managed a patronizing laugh before Daniel grabbed him by the throat. Thomas's eyes darkened and the sound became deeper, throatier, as he snarled at Daniel.

"If you remain with the wolves our paths will inevitably cross again," Daniel continued. "I am giving you one chance. Do not squander it. Leave the pack. The scent is fresh on you. The easiest time to get out is now." He released the boy.

They walked back to the house together, where Thomas said his goodbyes to Joshua, Nora, and Susan. Joshua offered to let him stay, saying it was too dangerous to go out alone, but Thomas said his mother had become very ill and he could not be away from the house for long. As he passed through the gate he looked back for a final glance at Susan. Then his gaze turned to Daniel.

"Till our paths cross again," he said, and walked off into the darkness.

Daniel stayed under the front awning, watching the break in the trees which led to the road Thomas had taken. He puffed away at his pipe, lost in thought, not bothering to turn when Susan came out. After several minutes he decided to break the silence, not sure why she had come to join him.

"You should be an actress," he said, looking at her.

"Why do you say that?" she asked.

"Your love of stories, your enthusiasm when you tell them… and the way you play that young man like a fiddle," he pointed with his pipe in the direction Thomas had gone.

"I'm sure I don't know what you mean," she said, blushing.

"I imagine there are many young men in town who think they are fishermen, reeling you in. The truth is you're not hooked. You just tug the lines for fun."

"Or maybe I'm just waiting for some fisherman to use the right bait," she countered, with a girlish smile.

Silence returned and Daniel puffed on his pipe, not releasing the stare he held with her. Her eyes were a deep green, just as his wife's had been. They held a youth and an innocence all too familiar. Daniel couldn't tell if it was inappropriate to look at her with such intensity but he found himself not wanting to look away. She didn't seem to mind. For a moment, he thought he saw his wife.

"I saw a play once when I was a little girl," she continued. "It was the first real story I had heard other than my mother and father's bedtime stories. There was a woman."

She looked away as if lost in some dream. "A beautiful woman who played the princess, Jesure. That's when I realized it."

"You wanted to be an actress?" Daniel asked.

"I wanted to be Jesure," she said, looking to the ground. "I wanted to live in a world where no matter how bad things got, there would always be a happy ending."

Daniel had felt the same way many times when he was a child. Over the years he had often wondered whether it was the beautiful innocence of childhood that had made him so drawn to wonder and joy or whether it was just adolescent naivete. He had never come to a conclusion.

"But that's obviously not real," she continued, blushing. "I would settle for being an actress, traveling the world, pretending to be in a fairy tale wherever I went."

"The world is filled with pain; though there is no escaping it, it is filled with joy as well." Daniel wasn't sure why he had said it. In fact, he didn't even know if he believed it. But it seemed to help as the pensive look fell away from her face and her smile returned.

They stood for some time in silence, listening as the first drops of rain fell to the ground.

"I never did thank you for getting me out of the romantic sunset gaze tonight," she said.

"It was getting late. Your mother didn't want you out all night," he replied.

"I'm sure," she said. She turned to leave and then paused as if remembering something.

"I think Thomas was going to kiss me tonight. You interrupted, and he didn't get the chance. So I guess this belongs to you." She walked up to Daniel and, standing on her tiptoes, kissed him on the cheek.

Daniel remained motionless as her lips brushed against his cheek. The last kiss he had ever received had been many years ago, a gift from his wife. He should have thought of her, but he didn't. He remained lost in the moment this beautiful young woman had initiated, appreciating every tiny detail of it. The touch of her skin, the warmth of her breath, the scent of her hair as it brushed by him. A brief image flashed through his mind in which he was kissing her back, not on the cheek but on the lips. Like the tiniest drop of blood into water, it tainted his mind. The thought had been so brief, hardly detectable, and now he could not get it out.

She pulled away from him, smiling, looking at him with those mysterious eyes once more before turning and leaving him to his pipe. Daniel fingered the last of his tobacco, debating whether to save it or finish it. After several moments of deliberation he reloaded his pipe and, after lighting it, turned back to the rain, wishing it could wash away all of the things on his mind.

A low growl rose through the downpour of rain, waking Daniel from his sleep. It could have been a low rumble of thunder or maybe the ghost of Roland trying to warn him. Either way, he was awake now. His head felt heavy and foggy. He had only been able to drift in and out of sleep. He rose from his blankets, which he had placed by the door, drawing his sword as he did so. He waited, listening. Light rain pitter-pattered on the ground.

Then he heard it again. Like a lion stalking its prey, he moved through the doorway out into the rain, following his instincts, brandishing his sword. There was nothing. The rope tethered to the bucket at the well groaned eerily as it swayed back and forth. Then came a roar like a thunderous crash shaking the ground. The sounds of pigs squealing flooded his ears, and he ran blindly through the downpour towards the sty. As he stepped into the pen he could feel the beast moving around him, invisible behind a wall of rain and a cacophony of sounds. Then it all stopped. The rain ceased, and by the light of the moon, Daniel saw he was standing in the pigsty. The pigs had gathered around him, and now stood oddly still as though he were their leader and they stood at attention, awaiting his orders. Daniel spun, searching, but there was no beast to be found. He looked down to see the blonde strands of hair mixed in the mud, the freckles of blood blushing her cheeks. He looked down to see the face of his dead wife staring back at him.

Daniel snapped awake, covered in sweat, drawing his sword on instinct. He rose from his makeshift bed by the door, his heart racing, and stepped out into the gray-white fog. It had been raining as he drifted off to sleep, and now in the early hours of the morning a fog had begun to rise with the sun. Something was wrong. He could feel it. He could taste it. He could smell it. Following along the rail of the pigsty, he noted the silence. It was the type of quiet that follows the end of some grand performance, like when an audience sits in silent awe just before the eruption of applause. A copper-like scent filled the air, and Daniel knew it was the smell of blood filling his nostrils. He opened the gate to the sty and found the pigpen littered with entrails. The wolf had returned. Daniel made his way through the pigpen, counting how many of the swine had survived the attack. In the end he deduced five pigs were missing and was relieved to find he did not see his dead wife among them.

The air seemed to sit motionless and thick as the temperature and humidity increased. The fog had lifted, and Daniel and Joshua had spent the better portion of the day cleaning out the pigsty. The children had been quarantined inside the house with their mother so as to not see the aftermath of the attack. When they had finished, Daniel and Joshua had fed the pigs and gone to the river to wash. They returned late in the day.

"What's wrong?" Nora asked, seeing the pained look on Daniel's face.

"I have to go," Daniel said.

The whole family froze. Bella ran over from her mother's lap, grabbing Daniel's leg.

"But you pwomise I no get eated!" she reminded him.

"And you won't," he said, hugging Bella. "But that is why I must go. I have to find the creature who did this," he said to the rest of the family. Joshua seemed to understand this decision. Daniel could see the tears welling up in Susan's eyes, but she held them at bay.

"Are you going to kill it?" Isaac asked.

Daniel wasn't sure how to answer, as the children were young; but they also deserved to know that no monster would come looking for them because there would be no more monster.

"Yes," he said.

"Will you at least stay for supper?" Nora asked.

"I really should be on the road," Daniel replied.

"Please," Nora implored him. "Just share one more meal with us."

Daniel looked around the table at this family he had come to know and love. He knew he should leave, but even as he heard the words he knew he wanted nothing more than to stay. That is when he saw her. Her bloody hair matted to her face, hands on the table, revealing the marks the wolf had left on her. She sat with dead, motionless, eyes in the seat Susan was supposed to be in. Daniel shuddered.

"Daniel?"

Daniel looked at Joshua, who had called his name.

"Alright," he replied. "But only for dinner." He looked back to the far end of the table. His wife was gone.

After dinner, Bella and Isaac were put to bed by Susan. Nora and Joshua cleared the table, returning to Daniel when they finished.

"You came to us so suddenly and now you wish to leave in the same manner," Nora said as she reclaimed her place at the table.

"That's the flow of life. People come and go just like the seasons. We must appreciate them while they are with us," Daniel answered, unable to meet her eyes.

Joshua sensed Daniel was not giving them the whole truth.

"Only time I've ever seen a man get up and leave so quickly as you intend to was when he had a posse on his tail. What are you running from, Daniel?"

"You have been so kind to me." Daniel began before pausing, unsure of how to continue. He did not wish to frighten them. "As I am sure you both know, my wife was killed by a werewolf... and I still see her. She only appears to me when there is danger. When a werewolf is close by." He watched them as he finished, "When death is close by. I saw her on the shore of the river the day we met. Roland was the victim."

Joshua and Nora took a moment to process the information.

"So you are leaving because you no longer see your wife?" Joshua asked.

"No," Daniel said. "I'm leaving because I saw her tonight. If I leave I can hunt the beast. Take the fight to him. If I stay... Castles under siege are at a disadvantage."

"Where is the last place you saw your wife?" Nora asked.

Daniel's eyes betrayed him. He couldn't help but glancing over to Susan's spot at the table. He rose to leave but Nora stopped him once more.

"You may leave in the morning, Daniel," she said. "You have worked a full day, and you are distraught. You cannot hunt anything in your condition."

Daniel looked to Joshua, who nodded in agreement.

"Alright," he agreed. He took out his pipe and made his way out the front door.

The night came and went without bringing sleep to Daniel. He sat with his back against the wall, chewing his empty pipe, his mind lost in a memory. Sheep's wool had scraped up against his skin. The dry chalky dirt had powdered his hands as he waited with patience under the gaze of the hot sun. There had been a light breeze tugging at the tall grass that had surrounded him, and in the distance the sound of

147

cowbells. He had waited for hours. Then out of nowhere it had come to him: the sense of imminent danger. He had gripped his sword tighter, barricading any fear into the furthest corners of his mind. The ground had started to rumble beneath his fingertips. The werewolf was charging him. It had been a soft rumbling at first, then harder and more distinct with each bound. Then nothing. The wolf had lunged and Daniel rose, brandishing his sword. The beast's jaws had been open wide with razor teeth ready to devour him. The sword's tip had gone straight through the beast's chest, piercing the heart. The wolf had been dead even as it toppled onto Daniel, almost crushing him with its sheer weight.

Daniel had lain there on the ground for a long while after his first kill. He remembered the blood and saliva that had covered him, staining the sheep's wool. He remembered the shaking in his hands as the adrenaline surged through him, pounding in his head as if it would burst. But most of all, he remembered the smell. It had been the first time he had caught the scent of the werewolf, and it had been sweet and intoxicating.

Daniel awoke, not knowing when his thoughts had slipped into the brief dream. It was dawn. Light tremors shook his hands, and he reached for his pipe before remembering he had used the last of his tobacco. He cursed under his breath, closing his eyes and taking a deep breath of the humid summer air. He heard the latch on the door open, and he turned to see Susan creep out of the house.

"Daniel, did you sleep outside?" she whispered, not wishing to wake the others.

"Didn't do much sleeping," he answered, getting up and brushing himself off.

"Are you alright?" she asked, concerned. "You don't look very well."

"I'm fine," he answered, the tremors in his hands

getting worse. "Would you walk with me?"

"Of course," she answered, taking his arm in hers. The thought of kissing her returned. He began walking out into the tall grass. He took each step with determination, heading in the direction of Roland's grave.

"Daniel, what's wrong?" Susan asked.

His breath had become labored, and his eyes moved erratically back and forth as if searching for something, or perhaps trying to hide from something. He collapsed in the grass just before they hit the tree line.

"Daniel!" Susan cried. "Daniel! Don't move; I-I'll go get help!" Her panicked voice resonated in his ears. The light began to fade as Daniel's eyes closed, and he could smell her hair as the wind passed by. He could fight it no longer. Susan turned to go, but his hand caught her wrist. It was such a simple movement. It happened in less time than it would take for an acorn to fall to the ground. Yet it may as well have been an explosion. Susan looked at Daniel, disbelief flooding her face as realization rose within her. She watched as his eyes opened, no longer the eyes that she had come to know. Tears streamed down his face as it twisted in agony.

"Susan," he whispered. "Run."

His grip released and his body began to writhe, sharp pain cracking through him like lightning. Susan stood for a moment, frozen in horror.

"Run!" he growled.

Daniel fell to the ground, gasping for breath. He could not see her, but he could hear her, smell her. The wind still tore the beautiful scent from her and carried it back to where he lay. It intoxicated him and for a moment he wondered if it would drive him completely mad. Then pain coursed through him and his body began to transform.

Run, he thought. *Run!*

He realized he was running, not like a man but like a

hound. He did not know if he had meant it to be a command for himself or for her, but it was too late. He moved through the field with speed and precision. He could hear her sobs, her desperate gasping for breath, as her footsteps pounded away like a horse. The ground seemed to tremble beneath her. He could feel it. She was almost back to the house.

He dove over the tall grass like a lion, claws outstretched and jaws open wide. She lay frozen on the ground, paralyzed by fear. Everything seemed to move slowly and quietly. Then Joshua crashed into him.

Daniel hit the ground on his shoulder, rolling and landing on all fours. His claws dug into the smooth earth and he positioned himself to strike again. Then he saw the sword.

"You forgot something," Joshua whispered, brandishing the weapon before him.

The beast growled a deep low sound.

"I like you." Joshua said. "But make no mistake, I will kill you."

The beast looked away.

"That's right, Daniel," Joshua whispered.

The beast leaped back into the tall grass, darting back to the forest.

Despair ate at him like a worm moving slowly through an apple, first moving to its very core and then eating it from the inside out. In his youth he had followed his faith to the letter; but as he grew, evil had still managed to corrupt him, seeping through the cracks of his soul like water through the foundation of a citadel until it eroded and the walls collapsed. He did not know how far he had traveled. Time was distorted when he changed. Moving through the woods, looking for something, anything, on which to feed, and finding nothing, he had reverted to a man, or rather what was left of a man. He felt hungry and sick at the same time, as he stumbled forward through the woods, trying to regain his faculties like a drunk sobering up. His vision was no longer blurry, nor was his mind.

Oh God, he thought. *Oh God...*

Shame washed over him. He had almost killed her, and now everybody knew. They knew his weakness. They knew what he really was. He stumbled upon a clearing, and the heat of the day bore down on him. There was a small dirt hill with a dead tree. On one of the tree's lower branches hung a rope. Daniel stood panting at the foot of the hill. The hot sun seemed to dry out the dirt until he could breathe it in. Sweat dripped down his face, and he couldn't tell if it was caused by the intense heat or the pain of his transformation. Daniel took his first steps towards the tree. As he got closer he reached out, taking the rope, only one thought crossing his mind. As he lifted it, he saw it was already in a noose. Who had left it there, he did not know, but it seemed they had predicted his coming.

"It's a cursed tree," a voice called from behind him.

"I'm a cursed man," he answered without turning. He knew the sound of Joshua's voice.

"Is that how you have come to be a werewolf without being bitten?"

"The first wolf I killed by dressing as a sheep. The rest I killed by dressing as a wolf. You can only remain a sheep for so long when you live in the skin of a wolf," Daniel answered, tying one end of the rope firmly to the tree, testing it with his hands to be sure it would not break. He heard Joshua's footsteps approaching.

"How is she?" Daniel asked.

"She will be alright," Joshua answered.

Daniel turned to face him and was surprised to find Joshua had come empty-handed.

"Please know, Joshua, I never..." He couldn't finish the sentence. He had never wanted to hurt the girl? He had almost killed her. Had never wanted to hurt the family? He almost took part of it away. Had never meant to hurt his friend? Daniel's eyes began to glass over with water and a small stream of tears slipped away. He had believed he was a good man, and yet he had failed himself so many times. Now the illusion was broken. If he had ever been a man he was no longer. He was an animal, and he mourned the death of the man he thought he had been. He slipped the noose around his neck.

"No, Daniel! Wait!" Joshua protested.

"I am the one from the prison. I killed Roland!" he shouted. Then he choked in a sharp breath before groaning, "And I killed my wife."

"I know." Joshua stated.

"How long?"

"Since Roland died," Joshua answered.

"Why?" Daniel cursed. "Why did you let me stay? I could have killed you! Your family!"

"Because I knew if I sent you away, you would end up here." Joshua said, hands raised, showing he was only there to help.

Daniel looked at the noose and then at the tree.

"Maybe not at this tree. Maybe not for many years," Joshua continued.

"How did you know?" Daniel asked.

"I recognized the smell." Joshua chuckled. "It took a while, all of your tobacco drowning it out."

Daniel had smoked to dull his own sense of smell, but it had also masked his scent.

"You never quite forget the smell," Joshua continued. "Their scent calls to you until long after your loved ones put you in the ground," he finished, slowly pulling the top of his shirt down to reveal the teeth marks in his shoulder.

"You are a wolf?" Daniel asked in disbelief.

"I was. No more. Some men are truly monsters, others become monsters trying to ease the pain of the world around them. What pain did you wish to ease?"

Daniel's thoughts reeled out of control. He needed his pipe. He needed to smoke.

"All of it," he answered. "If death is the ultimate price then why does living cost so much?"

They both stood in silence. The sun had begun to set.

"There is freedom from your pain. But you cannot do it alone. Come with me," Joshua said, extending his hand.

"I can't," Daniel answered, the golden rays of the sun glinting off of his tearstained cheeks.

"You can."

Daniel felt his knees weaken. He was so close. The earth seemed to draw him closer, and if he let it, it would pull him down until it wrapped itself around him and he could sleep forever in its loving embrace. He took out his pipe and remembered there was no tobacco. He watched as it slipped from his shaking hand. He was so close. He would be able to sleep, he wouldn't need his pipe, and he would never be a monster again.

A deep fear set into Daniel. He had never been afraid to die, but this was different. He looked into Joshua's eyes, pleading.

"Please! Kill me!"

Joshua sighed and came close enough to touch Daniel.

"There is peace," he said, lifting the coarse rope from around Daniel's neck.

Daniel collapsed, shaking, into Joshua's arms, and Joshua held him as he wept, as if Daniel were his own son.

Dusk had settled as they returned to the farmhouse. Daniel and Joshua had spent almost an hour at the tree, discussing how Joshua had become a werewolf and how he had managed to become a man again.

"It wasn't easy and it sure wasn't from smoking," he had said. "And Nora played a big part in it too. She never gave up on me. It's something you just can't get through alone."

That part had resonated with Daniel. Even when his wife had been alive there had always been a piece of him that had felt alone. He felt exhausted and pathetic, and as they came to the open field he became aware he would have to see Susan. Fear and shame returned to him. *What would she say?*

"How are you feeling?" Joshua asked.

"Do you really want to know?"

"A warm meal and a good night's sleep will do wonders for you."

"I look forward to them."

As a piece of glass hits the ground and shatters into a thousand pieces, a terrified scream shattered the serenity of the moment.

"Joshua!"

Nora came running from the house, Bella in her arms and little Isaac in tow.

"Joshua!" she screamed. "Joshua!"

Joshua and Daniel broke into a mad dash. Joshua ran to his family, scooping them up in his arms. Daniel rushed past them into the house, ready to fight off any intruder who might have chased them out. After a quick sweep of the place he knew the danger had passed. He returned to Joshua, who was desperately trying to calm his wife, motioning for her to take long deliberate breaths. Nora sobbed in hysterics.

"Where is Susan?" Joshua asked.

"He took her," Daniel said, emerging from the house with his sword.

"Thomas?" Joshua asked, looking from Daniel back to Nora.

Nora nodded.

"Why?" he asked

"To get to me," Daniel answered, slinging his sword over his shoulder.

"I'm coming with you," Joshua stated.

"You have a family." Daniel said. "I may be a monster, but I am still the hunter."

"She is my daughter." Joshua said, pushing past Daniel and heading for the door. He was in the house for only a few moments before he emerged with a sword of his own. He strapped it through his belt, and it swung gently with each step. He approached Daniel, scooping up Bella, who hid her face in his shoulder.

"My brother lives in town. We will take Nora and the children to him. Then we will find Thomas."

The smell of tobacco overpowered the two men as they entered the sultry taproom. An old blind man sat in the corner strumming out a lively tune on his guitar, and the tiny room felt packed as many overdressed men danced with underdressed women in a small clearing between several tables. Sweat and spilled ale bathed the floorboards, which creaked underfoot, groaning as if pained by the abuse. To the left rose a staircase which led to a second floor of three bedrooms: one where the bartender slept and two where the girls made their living. On the far end of the room stood the bar.

At the furthest table a lone boy sat smoking a pipe, and the two men went straight for him, moving through the crowd.

"Where is she!" Joshua demanded, slamming the boy's head down to the table.

The blind man ceased fingering his guitar and the whole room stopped to see what the commotion was. The barman began to come around the counter, but stopped when Daniel drew his sword and held up its emblem for all to see. The barman nodded. This was the hunter's business. No one would interfere.

"Play your music," Daniel said to the guitarist, and the old man began to play again. A few guests continued their dance but many started to speak in hushed tones.

Thomas looked up at Joshua through drunken, lazy eyes. He started to laugh but then began to cry.

"I loved her," he choked, taking a deep breath before looking to Daniel.

Even through Thomas's half glazed eyes, Daniel could see hatred pour out of them like wine from a bottle.

"I could have controlled it. I could have controlled the beast for her."

Daniel knew what Thomas meant. *I know what you did. You almost killed her, just as you killed your wife.* He was trying to get inside Daniel's head. In spite of this knowledge, Daniel's mind did drift to his wife and to the illusion of control he too had held so many years ago.

"Where is she?" Joshua hissed. "I will not ask again."

"Dagon has her."

Joshua let go of the boy's head. Thomas sat up again, blood beginning to drip from the split right above his eyebrow. Thomas wiped it off with the back of his hand and licked it.

"Who is Dagon?" Joshua asked.

"Dagon is the leader of the pack," Daniel stated. "If he has your daughter-"

"A council has been called," Thomas finished.

"What does that mean?" Joshua asked.

"Six of the eldest wolves will be there, and they will sacrifice your daughter to the dark spirit," Daniel answered.

156

"Among other things," Thomas stated with a whimsical smile as he took another swig of ale.

Joshua's face fell.

"How do you know this?" he asked.

"Because he delivered her to them." Daniel said. "For a wolf to become a pack member he must offer human sacrifice. She was his tribute to the elders."

A look of realization crossed Joshua's face. Thomas could not meet his gaze.

"I swear if anything happens to her-" Joshua hissed into Thomas's drunken ear.

Daniel grabbed him by the arm, spinning him away from the boy.

"It is not good to make threats in barrooms. The boy is of no more use to us, and we haven't much time," Daniel turned to leave, Joshua close on his heels.

"Good luck, boys!" Thomas cackled, raising his glass in salute.

Large stone steps lay at the base of the mountain of sacrifice. The first half had been traveled by many, as people had begun the journey in search of unveiling the mysteries of the werewolf, but few had completed it. Daniel looked up to see two giant statues of werewolves looming over them: Mal and Bal, one on either side of the stone steps. It was said they were the first two werewolves to ever walk the earth. It was also said whoever passed these two statues would be forever cursed. The hair on the back of Daniel's neck rose.

"You don't have to be here," Daniel stated.

"Would you leave your daughter to the wolves?" Joshua asked.

"They will have begun." Daniel said, turning to measure the sun against the purple-blue horizon line. It was odd to see something so sublime in the face of such evil. He turned back to Joshua as Joshua looked at the statues of Mal and Bal.

"I am not familiar with the sacrificial ritual."

"They will have beaten her with oak switches," Daniel said, watching Joshua's eyes brim with tears. "The youngest of the council marks her, then the eldest of the council recites the curses. After which they will tie her to the altar in the center of the coliseum. They burn incense. As the sun falls, it burns lower and lower until the incense ignites the chaff at the base of the altar. The altar is stone so it will survive the fire. They recite the offering prayer, if you can call it that. After the sun has set and the moon is at its peak they will turn into werewolves and partake of the flesh -"

"That's enough." Joshua interrupted.

Daniel looked to the sun again, knowing they were losing precious time.

"I need you to know," he said, placing a hand on Joshua's shoulder. "I need you at your best up there. She will be bloody and bruised and marred. But she will live and she will heal. I need you to trust me."

"I do," Joshua answered with venom in his voice.

"No matter what happens up there, you get your daughter and get off of this mountain." Daniel said, drawing his sword and racing up the steps. Joshua followed.

As they reached the final steps the sweet smell of incense caressed and welcomed them. A drop of rain fell on Daniel's head, and thunder began to rumble in the distance. They stood at the entrance of an ancient, decrepit stone structure. Flashes of lightning cut through the darkness, revealing broken pillars and piles of rubble in spots where the ceiling had caved. A cold rain began to fall. The small warm light of a flame flickered just bright enough for Daniel and Joshua to see a figure tied to a stone altar. The flame burned low on the incense.

Daniel wasted no time searching the shadows. He charged in, sword raised, like a gladiator. Joshua followed close behind. Only the constant pitter-patter of the rain echoed against the stone. It became so rhythmic it was as if they moved in silence, and Daniel might have wondered if they were alone had he not been able to smell the elders.

Silent as a ghost, Daniel saw an unnatural movement on his right. He spun out of the way, slicing with his sword as he did so.

There was a scream and a hideous creature, half-man and half-wolf, fell to the ground.

"Dagon!" it screamed. "Dagon! Help me!"

Daniel left him, reaching the altar and frantically cutting the girl's bonds. Her head turned and she looked at him through half swollen eyes.

"Daddy?" she whispered.

"I'm right here," Joshua said, scooping her up in his arms.

Joshua looked to his sword, then Daniel.

Daniel nodded as realization came over Joshua. He had been so focused on Susan he hadn't realized he could not carry his daughter and fight at the same time. Daniel motioned for Joshua to follow him. Accompanied only by the dying creature's screams, they crouched low and made their way back to the entrance.

As they reached the top of the steps, Daniel froze. The screaming had stopped. A low growl came out of the darkness, and Daniel turned and rushed Joshua out of the structure and down the first steps. Joshua turned back.

"Go!" Daniel commanded.

Joshua nodded, turning and disappearing into the storm.

Daniel stood alone, facing the darkness.

There are only five now, he thought, but he knew the chances of killing five werewolves in the same fight would require a miracle.

"We can smell you," came a voice.

Daniel brandished his sword.

"You are one of us," the voice continued.

No, he thought, but he knew it was true. Then he wondered if a werewolf could fight five of its own kind.

"Why do you fight it?" the voice continued.

Daniel felt the sense of intoxication come over him again. He could smell the blood of the dead elder. His hair began to stand on end. His teeth ached and his body began to change. He wanted it. He wanted to feel that power flow through his veins once more; to escape the inevitable pain that was to come. Then he stopped it. If he was to die tonight, so be it, but he would not turn again.

Daniel stood staring into the darkness.

"Let's finish this, Dagon," he said.

A loud cry came from the darkness. It was an odd, terrifying sound. It was not a cry of power the way a war cry is strong to intimidate an enemy, nor was it a cry of joy the way a child might yelp when his father brings home a special candy treat. It was a cry of agony, the cry which escapes a man not when he has been tortured for days but for years. It was the cry a person gives when they give up.

The first wolf lunged out of the darkness, and Daniel dodged out of the way, slicing off the wolf's arm as he went. The creature tried to land on all fours but crashed due to its missing appendage. The wolf's momentum carried it over the wet stone and right over the edge of the mountain.

Another werewolf shot out of the darkness, slashing at Daniel's chest. One claw managed to find Daniel, right before he slid his blade cleanly between the beast's ribs. The wolf howled in pain and Daniel pushed it down the stairs. He walked down to it and decapitated it before it could rise again, ignoring the pain in his chest.

He turned back to the dark threshold of the ancient sacrificial chamber. *Three left*, he thought. He debated waiting outside, but he knew they would not come out. If he stood by the door, they would wait for him to fall asleep and then take him without a fight.

As he stepped through the threshold and into the darkness a terrible pain shot through his leg. The fourth werewolf bit him low, sinking its teeth in just above his ankle. Before he could respond he felt more teeth sinking into his shoulder, just below his neck, as the fifth wolf jumped on him.

Pain coursed through every inch of Daniel's body, and he fell. He knew he had to get up before both of his enemies climbed on top of him. Neither had released their bite and he knew their jaws would be too powerful to pry open, so he did the only thing he could think of. He grabbed the smallest finger on the claw of the one at his throat and yanked it backward as hard as he could. Immediately the jaws released as the werewolf yelped in pain and Daniel stuck his sword through its exposed neck.

The wolf biting his leg looked up just in time to see the blade pass through its partner's throat and then arc down. That was the last thing it saw.

Daniel winced in pain as the pressure on his leg released. He had decapitated the beast.

He tried to crawl away, fumbling around in the darkness. There was one left. *Dagon.*

He tried to stand, but fell and had to scramble to get his back against a wall. He sat and listened, once more on the floor in the darkness. He could make out the dark shapes of his surroundings, and he waited for movement. Outside the rain slowed, and Daniel could hear his own labored breathing. He touched the wound by his neck and knew he was running out of time. He tried to stand once more, holding the wall for support. He got his good leg under himself. The bitten one had become dead weight and the throbbing pain told him he would not be able to run or to fight. Daniel turned back towards the door only to find himself eye to eye with Dagon.

Dagon was a large, powerful werewolf, with muscular arms and old but dangerous eyes. He grabbed Daniel by the throat and heaved him up overhead.

"This doesn't have to be the end," he said. "Let the beast heal you. Hunt the man and his daughter with me."

Daniel wished Dagon had killed him. He closed his eyes, thinking of Joshua and Susan. Then he thought of Nora, Isaac, and little Bella. Such a wonderful little family he had been given the pleasure of knowing. He wondered what might have happened had he not been bathing in the river that day. Would Susan be on this altar, or would it have been some other poor girl? It all seemed so long ago now, and he felt the familiar pain, which had followed him for so many years after his wife's death, awaken within him again. The pain of being alone. But he was not alone. Death had come for him unless he returned to the beast.

He took a deep breath, Dagon's scent filling his nostrils.

"Yes," Dagon whispered.

Daniel shoved his sword through Dagon's heart and crumbled to the floor in a heap as Dagon released him.

The last elder stumbled about, groaning, trying to pull the blade out. Then he fell over, dead.

Daniel lay on the floor as his blood and life seeped out of him. After taking a moment to catch his breath he dragged himself to a section of the structure where the roof had collapsed. There he lay with his face towards the sky, letting the gentle rain cool him.

Pain. He thought. *Why does life have to hurt so much?* No man could escape it whether rich or poor, guilty or innocent. Daniel remembered the pain he had caused as the wolf and he shuddered. *Maybe*, he thought, *maybe this pain is my penance. My way of atonement.*

He smiled for a moment as he thought of Joshua carrying Susan. They had done it. The family would be safe now.

He watched the moon peek through a dark cloud as if it were the eye of some god, demanding to look upon his creation.

"What is your name?" he whispered, closing his eyes. "Why? Why did you let me become a monster?"

When he opened his eyes he saw a woman standing over him. She crouched down next to him, touching his face. She looked at him, without a word. Only a smile. The type of smile a parent might give, when their child is crying over something insignificant. It was not a smile of patronization, nor a smile of cruelty. It was a smile of joy and love, a smile which shows a fascination with the innocence of a child.

Tears began to build in Daniel's eyes.

"I'm sorry," he said, touching his wife's hand.

"I forgive you," she said, embracing him.

Then she led Daniel into the light of the moon to a place with no pain and no darkness.

THE DEMON OF
ST. JUDE'S ABBEY

5

Princess Marianna awoke, her head resting on a snow-white pillow. The bed upon which she lay was comfortable yet foreign. A warm blanket wrapped snugly around her like a cocoon. Her fingertips traced patterns in the soft fabric, searching to identify it. It was a blanket, but it was not *her* blanket.

As she sat up in the bed, candles cast an amber light, illuminating the vast, unfamiliar room. Elaborate tapestries decorated the walls, giving the place a regal but comfortable feel. A large dresser, handcrafted from a dark wood, stood against the far wall, accompanied by a desk and mirror. The left wall presented a large oak door; the right, shutters of a window.

Marianna slid off the bed, releasing the blanket only enough for her to walk. Her bare feet touched the cold stone floor. Without hesitation she went for the shutters, taking the blanket with her. A gust of icy spring wind greeted her as she threw them open. The soft light of the moon cast shadows on her face through the grated window. It was a clear night, and the surrounding moors were bare before her gaze. A distant castle loomed on the horizon.

As she closed the shutters and moved to the door, she felt an eerie feeling come over her. The door towered before her, nearly twice her height. A large metal latch and bolt hung on the right. She paused for a moment, observing the room a final time. Everything seemed to dwarf her, and she began to wonder if she had somehow awoken in the home of a giant. Returning her attention to the door, she struggled to slide it open just enough to peek through. Its weight was no surprise. She felt much colder now in spite of the blanket decorating her. Then, opening the door further, she stepped out into the darkness.

She descended a dark stairwell, which in turn led to a corridor. Light penetrated the stained glass windows lining the left side of the hallway, casting blotches of dark blue-green colors on the wall. *What a curious place*, she thought as she passed through. *I wonder to whom it belongs? And how did I end up here?* She exited the corridor, entering a large open room. Marianna noticed how the painted faces in the larger windows seemed to watch her. Moonlight shone through them, providing a dim light to what appeared to be a sort of dining hall. Marianna scanned the room, letting her eyes follow the columns up to a surrounding balcony and the shadowy ceiling rafters beyond. *What is this place?* she wondered. At the far end of the room stood a door with a large wooden bolt which, she guessed, would require at least three men to move. Whoever lived here did not want unexpected company dropping in. As she approached the center of the room, she noticed the floor for the first time. A massive emblem had been painted over the stone with an inscription beneath it. She recognized the image. It was St. Jude. At the sight of it, she began to draw a memory out of the fog in her mind. Guards had been transporting her to a neighboring kingdom. They had told her the legend of a nearby abbey, cursed by a demon. It had been the Abbey of St. Jude. Marianna stumbled backward at the thought.

"It's just a legend," she whispered, trying not to panic. She remembered stories as a child from her father. Stories about the vampires he and his friends had hunted. *We hunted those demons down like dogs*, he would say, *and we killed every last one of them.* She sat down and curled up, wrapping her arms tightly about her knees in silence. She tried not to think. She tried not to cry. It was already too late; the fear had set in.

"I see you are awake," thundered a voice from above.

Marianna almost screamed.

"Yes," she responded, curling up tighter. "Who are you?"

"The master of this place," came the harsh reply.

Marianna tried to see the speaker, but the upper levels were far too dark. "Do you have a name?" she asked timidly.

The voice paused, leaving a silence so deep Marianna began to wonder if she had imagined the whole thing.

"Jude," the voice sounded less menacing. "And you?"

"Marianna," she replied.

"Well, Marianna, You may roam about as you please."

"Please," Marianna cried. "I have to leave!"

"Why?" Jude asked, and for a second Marianna believed he might let her go.

"Please! My father is a king. He will give you much gold for my safe return," she bargained, beginning to cry.

"Do you know who I am?" he roared. "Have you not heard the legends! What would I possibly want with gold?"

"What do you want with *me*!" Marianna screamed through a steady flow of tears.

Silence.

"Amusement. You are my pet, human," he finished.

The words echoed in Marianna's ears, as her eyes closed and frightening thoughts began to haunt her. Like a child lost in a nightmare, running blindly from a force which could only be described as evil by nature, she could not see it, but she could feel it. She could feel him, an unseen presence, stalking her. She yearned to wake herself, to end the horrifying dream she had somehow found herself inside of. Her eyes shot open to see the shadows dancing around her. Her senses heightened. Closer, closer, he was coming. She could take it no more.

The next thing she knew, Marianna was bolting back to her bedroom, sprinting for the window. She had to get out. He was coming. She could sense him. The shutters slammed harder then she expected, scaring her, as she tore them open. She grabbed at the metal grate, letting it press into her skin as she shook it hysterically. It didn't budge. An anguished sound escaped from her lips as she sunk to the floor. She turned to the door, facing the dark void, waiting for him to come out and step into the pale light of the moon.

When Marianna's tears ran dry, the monster had still not come for her. Mustering up what little courage she had left, she crawled towards the door, not once letting her eyes off the darkness. Using the last of her strength, she pushed the door shut as quickly as she could, sliding the bolt to lock it. Feeling as safe as the room would permit, she collapsed onto the bed, exhausted, and drifted into a disturbed sleep.

Rain battered Jude as he sat along the edge of the abbey roof, his back resting against the wing of a stone gargoyle. He turned his head towards the sky, eyes closed, letting each drop of water pour through the lines in his face like tears. He sat there for hours, regardless of the weather. The torrents of rain did not disturb him in any way. No amount of water could quench the rage which had festered in his heart for so long. A look of pain crossed his face as he let his mind drift back to that night. The night he had lost everything. He had been offered a choice, and he had chosen wrong.

He ran his claws gently over the wet stone in frustration. *So many years lost*, he thought. *All for one stupid night.* He looked down into the fog, off the edge of the abbey, wondering if he would survive the fall. Banishing the thought from his mind, he left his perch and began walking along the ledge. He smoothed back his thick hair, running his fingers through it. His mother had stroked his head when he was a child and he had hated it. The thought now pained him. Years had passed, and he wondered what she would look like if he could see her again. He wondered what humanity looked like, and then his thoughts fell to Marianna.

She had been beautiful, not broken: an angel in the house of the demon. He laughed at the thought. She was a pretty girl and had a magnificent future ahead of her, a future Jude knew he would never have. Soon this would all be over. She would live happily, forever ignorant of the reality of the monster whose clutches she was now in. Then maybe he would be at peace.

He had waited long enough. No one would come for her tonight. He crossed the roof and dropped back down onto a ledge, entering his room through the window. He put on fresh clothes and his cape, pulling up the hood as he liked it. Then he retrieved a parchment and quill, writing out his invitation. He was almost out the door before realizing there were no clocks in the abbey, only a golden pocket watch that he kept in his pocket, and another copper one in his desk. He took the copper one from the desk before second-guessing his decision. *Would she prefer the gold?* he wondered. He stood for quite some time, debating with himself, until he realized just how ridiculous he was being. He slid the copper watch into his pocket, placing the gold one with the note. He looked around to be sure no one had witnessed his decision, though it would be impossible.

He left his room, moving through the shadows of the abbey until he found himself before her door. He reached for the door handle but stopped. He stood, silent. Something was different. This was not his room anymore. She was in there, sleeping. It would be wrong to enter. He reached for the door handle again, disregarding the sudden qualms. A gentleman would not enter. But he was not a gentleman, he was a monster. This was his house. She was not a friend or a visitor. Even if she had locked the door, Jude had a key. Looking down at the invitation and the pocket watch he carried, he stopped and stepped away from the door, releasing the handle in frustration. For a moment, he wished he had never kidnapped her.

Why? was the first thought that passed through Marianna's head when she woke to the sound of rain. The last thing she remembered was being on a journey. A journey which would bring her to a new life, a new kingdom, and her beloved. Guards were escorting her to the kingdom where she would be wed. She had fallen asleep in the carriage only to wake up in a nightmare. She had been taken by a monster, and in spite of what he had told her, she refused to believe this was for amusement. What could he possibly need her for? No matter, her Prince would come for her. She smiled at the thought.

Terror, once again, came over her as she turned to the door, noticing the two objects on the ground. *He was in here!* was all she could think. *He was in here while I slept!* Her eyes hurt from crying, but she could still feel the tears welling up again. Hot anger rose from her very core and spread through her. She dismounted her bed and picked up the objects, examining them. The first was a small golden pocket watch on a thin chain. She wasn't familiar with how it worked, but she knew her father had used one to keep appointments. The second object was a piece of parchment with writing on it.

Marianna studied it, feeling the hot tears bubbled over again. The fancy script looked pretty to her, but she knew no amount of staring would change her inability to read. Had she been able to read she would have seen the words:

Dinner will be at five o'clock, if you care to join me.

Frustrated, she placed them both on her bed, as she went over to search the dresser for something more appropriate to wear than a nightgown.

The dresser did not provide her with many options. This was not her castle; it was a former abbey and it was rare an abbey had to accommodate a princess. All of the clothes were old worn things the monks had collected for the poor. There were five dresses in total, two of which were too large for her and one that had been damaged beyond repair. Marianna looked at the two passable options and decided to go with the one she believed to be prettier. After changing, she draped the watch around her neck and checked it one last time. Then she picked up the note and headed for the door.

Marianna's day consisted of a thorough search of the first floor of the abbey. In the light of day, she found everything to be smaller than she had originally thought. Her room was rather large but seemed to have been designed for guests. She found several much smaller plain bedrooms, which had been for the monks. There was a dining hall with a kitchen attached, and Marianna imagined monks in brown robes sitting at the long table, sharing a meal. She continued on to find a food storage closet, where she helped herself to some bread and cheese. Leaving with an apple in hand, she continued on to the main door. She studied it for nearly an hour before accepting there was no way for her to move the bolt without help. She was trapped. Resigning herself to her fate, she entered the final room, a small chapel with candles, an altar, and a crucifix.

She also discovered a door to an outside garden but was discouraged to find it surrounded by a wall far too high for her to climb. She stayed outside until the day grew late; then she began her way back to her room.

As she passed through the main hall on the way back to the pantry, a mouthwatering aroma enveloped her. She followed it down into the dining hall, which was far different than she had left it. There were now candles all about and a fire in the hearth. The table held a dinner spread fit for a king, and at the far end of the table sat the figure of a man. He wore a thick black cape with a hood, which cast a shadow over his face in the candlelight.

"Thank you for joining me," he said. "I was beginning to think you were not coming." He rose and approached her with the prowess of a lion. He was tall, at least a head taller than she was. He stood up straight like a gentleman and appeared to have been brought up with manners, in spite of his dark exterior. She watched him, but still could not see under his cowl. She noticed his sleeves extended past his hands, hiding them from her gaze, as he pulled out the chair and motioned for her to sit. He returned to his chair in silence. She glared at the creature and, though she could not see his eyes, sensed he was staring back. She reached into her pocket and, removing the note, she broke the silence.

"What is this?" she demanded, holding up his note.

Jude stared at her, confused. "My invitation."

"To what?" she pressed.

"To dinner."

Marianna gracefully shielded her eyes with her hand at the realization. She felt stupid.

Sensing her embarrassment, Jude walked around the table. He pointed to the first word in his invitation, which lay beneath Marianna's gaze. She studied the long black fingernail with which he pointed.

"What does this word say?" he asked in a gentle tone.

Silence.

"You don't know how to read, do you?" he asked.

"No," she stated, brushing away a tear. "No, I don't."

"That's a good quality," he replied. "You are not afraid to admit your faults."

174

"Show me your hands," she retorted.

Jude hesitated. Then he held up his hands, letting his sleeves fall to his elbows. His hands looked more like a dragon's claws than hands. The backs appeared reptilian with thick, scaly skin. The insides were a softer tissue. His nails were long and black, glistening in the candlelight. After a moment, Jude dropped his hands, letting his sleeves descend once more over his abnormality. He returned to his seat, and they ate in silence, each lost in their own thoughts. Marianna tried to act as though this was all normal, but she knew it was not working. Nothing about this was normal. They were neither old friends nor lovers. They were hardly acquaintances.

"This was delicious," Marianna commented, trying to be polite.

"You speak in the past tense, insinuating you are finished and wish to be excused. Very well, you may go. It's not like you can go very far."

Taken aback, Marianna rose from her seat. "You are an insufferable creature! Make no mistake, I will be free of you! My Prince will come for me," she said.

"I'm counting on it," he answered.

"Then you wish to kill him?"

"No."

"Then why would-"

"Will you please be quiet!" he demanded, slamming his hand down on the table. He took a moment to collect himself before apologizing. "I'm sorry. I seem to have forgotten my manners."

"It's fine," she responded. "You are a monster. It's amazing you have any at all." She had almost made it to the door.

"Wait," Jude commanded. "I'm sorry. Thank you, for joining me."

Marianna left.

Marianna returned to her room, and gliding across the cold stone floor, she jumped onto her bed and melted into the covers. For a moment she felt relief as the problem she faced began to drift away. She closed her eyes and imagined she was back in her bedroom, sprawled on her bed, resting on a quiet summer day. For a moment she felt peace. After lying on her bed for a while, she rose, and finding a brush in her dresser, she began running it through her hair. She replayed the day's events in her head, considering all the things she had learned. Her thoughts turned to Jude. *The demon of St. Jude's Abbey,* she thought, remembering the legend.

Marianna put down the brush and approached the window, taking her pillow with her. The sun disappeared slowly, as though it were kissing the land goodnight. Marianna hugged the pillow and looked out at the castle in the distance. *My Prince is coming for me*, she thought, and hugged the pillow tighter.

Jude sat at his usual perch on the abbey roof, looking out at the distant castle. He had brought charcoal and parchment with him as he waited. Under the light of the moon he began to sketch out a picture of a woman. After several moments, he stopped and stared at his creation. Something was wrong. There was something about it he did not like. He must have made a flawed stroke, or perhaps several. He crumpled the image and tossed it off the edge of the roof. Ever since he had lost his humanity, he had never desired to draw people...until now. He set the charcoal piece down next to him, resting his head on his palms and sighing. His mind began to drift to thoughts of Marianna and the numerous possibilities of what the following day could bring. His eyes wandered once more to the castle on the horizon.

"Don't worry," he whispered. "This will all be over soon."

At the realization destiny would not come tonight he rose to leave. He looked down to see he had written her name on the abbey stone. *Marianna.* Feeling defeated and having little desire to do anything, Jude decided to go to sleep, in hope it might, in some way, bring him peace.

After making herself a light breakfast, Marianna began to wander through the second floor of the abbey. She found more bedrooms, a second kitchen, and a long foreboding hallway she assumed led to Jude's room. The last room she came upon was a library. It was a smaller room, but there was something very home-like about it. Each wall had bookshelves cut into it, and in the center lay cushions to sit on. In spite of the fact she could not read she felt a sense of comfort in the room. She walked along the bookshelf, running her fingers over the spines of the books.

"Magnificent, isn't it?"

Marianna jumped at the sound of Jude's voice. She had become so lost in her thoughts she had not noticed his presence. He watched her from the doorway, studying her.

"Do I frighten you?" he asked

"No," she lied. "Should I be afraid?"

"Your hands are trembling," he said, with a brief gesture.

"You startled me," she said, turning to the books. "What do they say?" she asked.

"Many things. It depends which one you pick."

Marianna walked to the wall before her and, after examining several books, took one from the shelf.

"What does this one say?" she asked Jude, handing it to him.

She watched the lower half of Jude's mouth, all that

she could see of his face, split into a smile. He opened the book with a profound reverence, examining the text as if it held a lifetime of memories.

"It is a story of a great hero, who gave up everything he had for the woman he loved, even his life. The gods looked upon his act of selflessness and gave him divinity," he said, shutting the book and handing it back to her.

"It sounds romantic," she said.

"It is. Every story is a lifetime you get to share and experience."

"That sounds wonderful."

"It can be. The key is to pick the right story."

"Have you read them all?" Marianna asked, observing how many books there were in the room.

"No, but I have read most of them."

The creature turned to leave but stopped at the door as though he had forgotten something.

"What's wrong?" she asked.

"Marianna," her name sounded beautiful when he said it. "Would you like me to teach you how to read?"

Marianna could not help but smile. "Would you?"

His answer surprised her.

"It would be an honor."

Marianna impressed Jude with her tenacity, and he found he could not take his eyes off her as she learned to read. He watched as she followed his instructions. He studied her face, though careful to hide his own, as she read aloud, laughing at her own mistakes. She was unnaturally quick to learn, and it was not long before she began reading by herself. They were only fairy tales and children's books, but they were still books.

Her face would shift from a look of intense concentration

into the most childish expressions as she deciphered the meaning of each word. Jude noticed her attraction to stories of adventure and romance, understanding her love of these things, for he had once felt the same way.

"Do you believe in true love?" he asked her.

"You mean a love like in the stories?" Marianna looked up from the book she was reading and smiled. She thought of her Prince, and it seemed as though she emitted a warm glow. "Yes."

"Really?" Jude asked, cynically. "You think a man could feel that way towards a woman?"

"Oh Jude, it's so much more than a feeling, it's a choice. It's not a destination. It's a journey." She paused, trying to find the right words. "Every day you wake up beside them, choosing them again and again over everyone else. Someone who would slay dragons to rescue you. I thought you of all people would understand. You love these stories."

"I *loved* them," he corrected. "Then one day I realized they were just that, stories. I have come to acknowledge the reality of human mistakes."

"You're fooling yourself. I can tell. You believe in love," she said, smirking at him.

"And your Prince?"

"I hope he does."

"Well, I am afraid I have no dragons at my disposal. He will just have to settle for me."

Jude rose to leave.

Marianna sat in frustration. She had found beneath Jude's appearance lived a very charming man. It seemed to her the creature would not allow himself to be happy, and she often wondered why. She tried to get him to laugh, and on occasion she succeeded, but it never lasted. He treated her as a gentleman would treat a lady. When he spoke, he spoke gently to her and with intention. Marianna loved his voice. She would lie on the cushions listening to him read, and she would often wonder if there were any sound so beautiful in all the world. The more time she spent with him, the more he seemed to be human. So why had he taken her? Why did he hate the Prince so much?

"What did he do to you?" she begged.

Jude ignored her question. Still fascinated with her beliefs, he asked once more.

"You really believe in love?"

"I do."

Jude left.

At night, Marianna stared out her window, desperately wishing she could see the castle through the thick fog that had set in. The late hours had not brought her rest. Instead her mind raced, questioning why her beloved had not yet come for her. Days had turned into weeks and weeks into a month. With each passing day she would have to find a new answer to the question: why hadn't he come? She told herself the journey was a long one. She told herself he had spent the weeks gathering knights to come for her and would soon be there. But tonight she had nothing. Tonight she was alone.

Wrapping her blanket around herself for warmth, Marianna left for the chapel. When she arrived, she was surprised to find Jude was already there. She turned to leave, not wanting to interrupt him, when he called to her.

"The things that keep us up at night are often worth praying about."

She entered the chapel, joining him in his pew. He could always sense her presence. He hadn't even looked up.

"I didn't think vampires prayed," she stated.

"I don't believe they do."

"But-"

"I am not a vampire," he answered. "Nor was I always like this."

"What happened to you?" she asked.

"I was once a prince," Jude said, his eyes reflecting the candlelight through an intense stare. "I became sick of formalities. I hated my duties and the rules I had to follow. One night was all I wanted, one night to do whatever I wanted. A devil was passing by my window the night I said that. He seemed to be a jolly, skinny little man. He was a bit like a court jester and always wore a smug little smile on his face. He told me he could give me a disguise that would conceal me for one night. He said the only catch was I would have to accept the consequences of my actions as a man. But I was a prince, I was *above* men. After very short consideration, I gave in.

"I went out to the town that night. No one recognized me. I lied, cheated, cursed, and gave in to my every desire. All for just one night. At the end of the night, I went home and tried to sleep, but I realized what I had done was wrong. I kept trying to convince myself it was only one night and it wasn't that bad. I fell asleep. When I awoke, I saw the transformation and the consequence of what I had done. My eyes had gone black from all I had seen. My teeth turned to fangs for everything I had said. My hands became claws for all I had done. My father came at the sound of my scream, but he didn't recognize me. He thought I was a demon who had devoured his son in the night. I came to this abbey for sanctuary. Even the monks fled in fear. I am a monster; the shadow of a man, long gone. It is ironic the abbey is named after Saint Jude."

"You are not a lost cause," Marianna said. "Jude is not your real name, is it?"

"No, I took the name Jude in hopes the saint would have pity on me and save me, but he hasn't."

"Perhaps he has, and you just haven't seen it yet."

Marianna could tell she had made Jude uncomfortable.

"And what is it you pray for tonight?" he asked.

"I came to pray for my love," she answered. "It seems he has forgotten me."

"He will come," Jude answered, looking away.

"I hope so," Marianna said, closing her eyes and breathing in deep. She found it odd, but there was something about Jude saying it that made her feel reassured. Again, her mind raced with questions. Why had Jude taken her? What did he hope to gain?

"Why did you do this, Jude?" she asked.

Silence.

Marianna opened her eyes to find she was alone.

The castle loomed on the distant horizon, tantalizing Jude's thoughts as the sun began to rise. Soon, very soon, this would all come to an end. Jude stood on the edge of the abbey roof, questioning his actions. In the beginning, everything had seemed so simple, so clear; but Jude had grown to appreciate Marianna's company, and now as their time together drew to a close, he couldn't help but wonder if he was doing the right thing. After all, he had made mistakes before. Jude tried to banish her from his mind. His choice was made and his fate was sealed the day he had chosen to take her. Soon the Prince would come. Soon.

As the sun rose in the sky, Jude left his perch to find Marianna. Standing alongside a pillar in the garden, he watched her move among the roses. He admired her grace and elegance. She looked to him as she lifted up a rose to smell it and smiled.

"Come join me," she called to him.

Jude had been careful to stick to the shadows and kept his face under the protective shade of his hood. He was afraid of what might happen if Marianna saw him in the light. He watched the golden beams of the sun run across her face. She closed her eyes and seemed to soak them in. He went out to join her.

"I love the sun," she said with a smile.

"And I love the rain," he stated, grimly. "They are like two lovers who cannot exist together."

"You're wrong," she replied. "Look!"

The few clouds overhead began to break, and they stood together in the rain and the morning light. She turned towards him, brushing back his hood and looking into his eyes. In the light she saw Jude was far more human than he believed himself to be. His eyes were not black, rather an incredible dark brown which held an overwhelming beauty as the sun shone through them. His face was beautiful, more so than most other men she had seen. Jude leaned forward until their foreheads touched. His lips brushed hers gently but she pulled away.

Jude stepped back, returning his hood to its place. He fled once more to the shadows of the abbey. She called to him, but he ignored her. The shadows were his protection; but they could not protect him from himself. Now he realized he had to confront all of the problems he had chosen to ignore. He had fallen for her, and there was no hope of them ever being together. He should have waited on the roof. She never should have been with him for so long. The Prince had still not come for her. Why had the Prince not come? Jude ran through the abbey to the roof and took his perch, his eyes sweeping the land.

Hours passed, and Jude knew the sun would begin to set soon. He refused to move. He did not want to see Marianna again. He could not let himself see her again. He sat on the edge of the roof, concealed in shadows, his black cape wrapped about him. He crouched low, making himself appear more like a gargoyle than a man. A small caravan approached from the woods. At last it was time. His problems would end and he would be free. The Prince had come.

Jude stood on the edge of the roof, waiting patiently. His hood masked his face, and a gentle wind tugged at his cape. At last the moment had come, the moment Jude had desired for what felt like centuries. He watched as the soldiers approached the abbey: eight soldiers and a cart, along with the one who led them, the Prince.

The Prince stopped, looking up at the dark figure.

"Vampire! I am in search of my Princess. She was taken from these parts. If you have any information as to her whereabouts or her captor, you may be handsomely rewarded," he called.

"I am the one you seek," Jude answered.

"I am here to negotiate terms," the Prince said, brandishing a purse of coins.

Jude's couldn't help but suppress a smile. This Prince did not desire to take unnecessary risks. Jude could admire that, but he would not let Marianna go without a fight. This was the moment he yearned for.

"Forgive me, I do not mean to insult you," the Prince continued with a smile. "It is such a small amount for so noble a prize." He snapped his fingers and two soldiers came forward carrying a treasure chest. The Prince opened it ostentatiously, letting its overflowing contents spill onto the ground. He stared up at Jude, waiting for a reply.

"Unless you fight me she will remain here." Jude felt his pulse begin to race. The moment was drawing near. Soon he would be freed of his hideous form.

"Why should we fight?" the Prince answered. "There is no need. You require more?"

He signaled to the guards and they brought out a slave girl of seventeen years. The child resisted as they thrust her forward and into the mud. She buried her face in her hands, terrified, crying out for her mother.

"Consider her a gift," the Prince waved. "Something for you to feed on."

Jude's eyes widened with outrage. He could not believe what he was witnessing. The Prince had waited weeks, enough time to raise a small army, and this is what he brought. Realization dawned on Jude, and he stood silently cursing himself for being so stupid. A fool for love would have come in three days, a cautious lover, in a week. No one truly in love would wait so long and bring so little. Fate had not come tonight, only a coward. Jude dropped from the roof, landing on the ground, a spider descending from his web. Before the Prince's guards could react, he had moved through them like a wraith and he had the Prince by the throat.

"Riches and rhetoric will not help you here," he growled. "Leave now. If you ever come back here I will kill you. If I hear, see, or smell your armies approaching, I will kill the girl and flee the abbey. I will hunt you and I will haunt you. You will never sleep, knowing I will be waiting in the shadows to steal your life away. Now get out."

As Jude turned to leave, he reached down and broke the slave's chains with his claws. "You are free now, go."

The Prince looked down at the treasure he had brought, shaking his head in disbelief. Then he looked to his guards, saying, "My duty is to my kingdom and its need for a successor. There are many princesses in the world. Pick up this mess and let us leave." With that they left.

Marianna sat on her bed, pressing her fingers against her lips. Jude had fallen for her. She wondered what it would have been like had she let him kiss her. She thought of her

Prince. She had imagined such happiness with him, but she had also been happy here with Jude. She didn't know what to feel, her heart torn and conflicted. Her Prince had not come to rescue her, but Jude was the reason she needed rescuing. She cared very deeply for both of them.

"Marianna!"

She heard him shout.

"Marianna!"

She decided she would tell him. The best thing to do was to be honest with each other. His actions had spoken for him. Now she needed to answer. She found him in the main hall.

"Jude, about the garden-" She began.

"Forget it. Your Prince has come," Jude interjected.

"He came?" Marianna asked, a wave of happiness sweeping over her.

"Yes, the door is open. If you hurry you may still catch him. Now go." Jude said, brushing past her.

Marianna took two steps towards the door before curiosity stopped her. "Just like that? You kept me for all this time just to let me go."

"Why I kept you is not your concern," Jude answered in frustration. "He is out there now! The man you have been waiting for! Go to him!"

"No! Not until I know why. Why did you take me?" she demanded.

Jude stood, his back to her, staring into the distant darkness.

"Answer me!"

His gaze on the floor, he responded, "It was in an act of selfishness that I became what I am. I thought maybe, just maybe, someone's act of selflessness would be enough to set me free." He turned his head to face her.

Marianna's heart broke at the realization of what he

186

had meant. She had been his token to the afterlife.

"You wished for him to slay you to rescue me. You desired to be killed in the name of love, just like the monsters in all of those stories."

"I never intended for any harm to come to you."

She stepped towards him.

"My first days here I believed you were a monster, a vampire bound for hell. But I was wrong. There is nothing farther from the truth."

Caressing his face, she continued, "You are no monster, Jude. You've just forgotten how to be a man."

A tear escaped Jude's eye, painting a path down his face.

"I have to go," she whispered.

"I know."

Marianna felt the voice of freedom call to her as she passed the threshold of the abbey and stepped outside. At the edge of the woods she looked back, wishing she could somehow ease Jude's pain. Then she began to run. Step after step she pressed forward, and she knew she wouldn't stop, not until she was in the arms of her beloved.

Jude watched her from the roof as she left the abbey to chase her dreams.

"How will I remember, without you?" he whispered to the wind. "I love you, Marianna."

Marianna walked down the dirt path which led away from the abbey. At first she had run, eager to be with her Prince, but she had grown tired and slowed to a walk. *Where is he?* She wondered. *How far away is he waiting?* She did not know where he and Jude had fought but couldn't imagine it had been much further. She tried to envision the encounter, a great battle ending with her Prince nobly sparing Jude's life.

Her thoughts were interrupted as a young girl ran out

of the woods towards her. She was muddy and her clothes were tattered. Mariana would have guessed her to be a slave girl, but she wore no chains.

The girl grabbed Marianna's wrist.

"My lady, you must run! It's not safe!" she implored.

"What are you talking about?" Marianna asked, gently freeing her hand.

"There is a demon in these woods," the girl said her eyes shifting back and forth. "A vampire!"

Marianna knew the girl had seen Jude; and if she had seen Jude, she had seen the Prince.

"Hush child, you are safe. He is not a demon, nor is he coming for you," she said. "Tell me where is the Prince, who fought him."

The girl began to cry.

"What's wrong?" Marianna asked.

"Don't take me back," the girl pleaded through her sobs.

"I already told you," Marianna said. "There is no demon."

"Don't take me back to the Prince," the girl cried.

A sick feeling formed in the pit of Marianna's stomach and began to spread through her. She felt warm and light headed. She reached for the girl's face with both hands and, after drying her tears, looked deep into the child's eyes.

"Tell me what happened," she said.

Jude descended into the abbey with a rage in his heart he had not felt since the day he had become a monster. He passed through his room, leaving claw marks across his door as he went. She had left. The agony began searing his soul shut. He would never again humiliate himself. He would never permit himself to hope. He would never love. He would never again be vulnerable. He would be a monster, and he would be stone. She had left. He walked down to the main hall. She had left. He fell to his knees and let out a cry of agony and rage. She had left.

A knock on the door pulled Jude from his thoughts. He knew it would not be her, but it could be. He ran to the door, nearly ripping it off of its hinges.

"Hello, Jude," said the little man.

Marianna stood alone on the path, the girl had left her some time ago. She had no tears left to cry. She felt foolish. Jude had been right. There were no knights in shining armor, there were only stories. True love was nothing more than a child's fantasy. Her Prince had shown up, and when money could not buy her from her captor, the Prince had left without so much as raising a sword. She felt disgust over the role the poor girl had been forced to play.

Now she sat on the hilltop overlooking her home. She no longer wished to return. If she did her father would force her to marry that snake of a prince.

But she did not have to return. No one knew she had escaped the abbey. She could find a nearby town and leave for another land. She would no longer be a princess. She was no longer sure she wanted to be one, though. She could go anywhere and be anyone just like one of the adventurers in the stories she had read. She closed her eyes. She could go anywhere now. She was free. Free of the abbey and free of her duties as a princess. *Where do I want to go?* she asked herself, but she already knew the answer in her heart.

"Jude! Jude!" Marianna called as she pushed through the doors and into the main hall. No one answered. The abbey felt empty. It felt cold. Marianna sank to her knees, no longer sure of what she should do. Her world crashed down around her. She had chased after a fantasy, and now she may have lost the thing she had sought all her life. What pained her most was the fact she had lied to herself. Deep down in the depths of her soul, she had known Jude loved her. The more she reflected on her mistake, the more she realized all she wanted was one more chance to love him.

Marianna looked up to see a little man step out of the shadows of the abbey. He bore signs of age, and his clothes were faded and tattered. He carried a walking stick, which he swung expertly around himself, reminding Marianna a bit of a clown.

"I'm sorry, Jude's a bit busy at the moment. Perhaps I can help?"

"I'm sorry, I didn't mean to intrude," she said, wiping her eyes. "I didn't know Jude had any visitors."

"Oh, it's quite alright. Come in," he replied with a low bow. "What's wrong?"

"It's nothing," Marianna answered.

"Clearly it must be something," he said, intrigued.

"A broken heart."

"In all of my travels I have yet to find a cure for that one," he answered with solemnity.

"Where are you from?" Marianna asked, quite charmed with the little man.

"A little bit of everywhere," he said, with a wink.

"My name is Marianna," she said, extending her hand.

Their introduction was interrupted by a mighty roar. Marianna looked up to see Jude leap down from the terrace. He landed between them and with one swift motion, sent the little man sprawling away.

Stunned by the sudden outburst of violence, Marianna reprimanded Jude. "What are you doing? He wasn't trying to hurt me."

Jude turned to Marianna, a look of fear in his eyes.

"You shouldn't be here!"

"And you should not attack your guests for-"

"That thing is not my guest," he interrupted, pointing to the little man. "That is the devil who turned me into what I am."

Marianna's face drained of all color as she watched the little man rise. He stared at her as he wiped a smear of blood from his lower lip. His face contorted into the most hideous, twisted smile Marianna had ever seen. Grabbing Jude's arm, she hid behind him as a child would her father. With one little smile this man had completely unnerved her. Jude stood between them, eyes glaring and fangs exposed.

"Well isn't this nice," said the little man.

"What do you want?" growled Jude. "Haven't you taken enough?"

"I haven't taken a thing," condescended the little man.

"You took my life!" Jude roared.

"Wrong!" the little man countered. "You did this to yourself! This was the price of your sin, a price which you agreed to. This was the consequence of your choice, from which I gained nothing."

"Then why are you here?"

"Because you owe me."

"For what?"

"For giving you the choice."

Silence.

The fear Marianna felt in the presence of this little man was nearly unbearable. She wanted Jude to hold her as he had done during the sun shower. She wanted to feel the security of his powerful arms around her. She wanted him to look her in the eyes and tell her everything was going to be alright. Marianna squeezed his arm but Jude pulled away, dropping to his knees.

"What do you want from me?" Jude asked in submission.

A smile crept across the traveler's face and his eyes flashed to Marianna.

Jude followed his gaze.

"She is not mine to give."

"Then we should have no conflict," he answered, seeming taller than before.

Marianna wrapped her arms around Jude, imploring him. "Please, Jude, it doesn't have to be this way!"

On his knees before the devil, Jude watched as his life passed before his eyes. He became overwhelmed with his sin, feeling its weight crushing him. He thought of Marianna. He thought of their time together, from the day they first met until the day the Prince had come for her. He thought of the dinners and the stories. He thought of the first book she had ever handed him, the story of a man who gave his life in an act of selflessness and was forever changed. *If a man can change for the worse than he must also be able to change for better.* Jude slowly lifted his eyes up to the little demon, who now towered over him.

"I will no longer submit to you."

The demon howled, stepping back as it transformed into a giant dragon. Marianna screamed as Jude grabbed her hand, leading her to the door. The ground shook with violent tremors and Marianna stumbled and fell. She looked into the beast's unforgiving eyes as its jaw opened to devour her. The dragon struck, but it was too late. Jude had grabbed Marianna, and they ran out into the night. The dragon let out a mighty roar.

Once outside, Jude stopped running and looked back. His face held a look of desperation. Marianna tugged his arm, urging him on, but he knew he could not. His past had caught up with him, and now it was time to face it. He looked to Marianna. Why had she come back? He took Marianna in his arms and kissed her.

"I don't know why you returned or how this will end. All I know is I love you, Marianna. And I have to do this."

Marianna pulled him close, kissing him again.

"Now go," he said.

She left at his bidding. Jude stood in silence outside the abbey, preparing himself to face the demon within. *One night can change everything.* The rain began to fall, and it resounded deep in the night.

A thunderous crash erupted as the dragon pushed through the wall of the abbey. The snakelike head began weaving back and forth searching for its prey. Catching sight of Jude, it let out a mighty roar.

Jude charged his opponent. Dodging the strikes of the great serpent's jaws, he leaped up onto its back. He tried to sink his claws deep into the monster, but its scales were like thick armor. He wrapped his arms around the base of the dragon's neck and began to squeeze fiercely.

The dragon roared again and slapped Jude away with its tail.

Jude crashed to the ground, gasping for breath. He barely managed to scramble out of the way as the dragon knocked over the abbey tower in an attempt to crush him. Dust and dirt rose in the air as the tower crumbled, and Jude used this cover to slip into the wreckage.

He could hear the dragon circling, brushing away stones with its claws and tail. He didn't have much time. He looked around frantically for a weapon and his eyes fell to the steel crucifix that had been mounted on the top of the tower as a steeple. It had snapped off and now looked like a jagged, half-broken sword. He picked it up, clutching it with both hands, before he stepped out into the open.

The dragon turned towards him. Jude charged. The dragon leaned back, preparing its final strike as the two looked intensely into each other's eyes, revealing their determination to destroy each other. Jude leaped and sunk the broken shard deep into the dragon's exposed chest. With a mighty roar, the dragon fell to the ground, the steeple piercing its heart.

Marianna heard a great roar and, fearing for Jude's life, ran back to the abbey. When she arrived, there was no dragon or monster, only a man.

WHERE MAN
AND MONSTER MEET

6

The truth is I am not a writer. I'm just a man who has a hard time dealing with reality. Someone once told me writing is like baring your soul for all to see. If that is true then I guess I have a need to bare mine.

The rain began to tap dance on my office window as a storm brewed in the distance. The humidity of the summer night had given birth to the beads of sweat which clung to me like leeches. I sat in my office, wanting nothing more than the sweet escape of a peaceful sleep. I closed my eyes, listening. The rain had begun to fall heavily and methodically. I confess, I was thinking about *her* again. I watched as the memories began passing through my mind like tiny ghost ships, haunting me.

In all of my work, I wished for nothing more than to create something beautiful, to weave these words into something beautiful. Perhaps that is the problem; perhaps there is no beauty in my soul to give life to these words. Perhaps after years of chipping away at it and surrendering its tiny fragile pieces, I no longer have a soul. That would explain why I feel something is missing, why in a world obsessed with the value of things I feel so unforgivably valueless.

A storm had begun to rage, not only outside my office but also somewhere in the depths of my being. There is a curse that comes with writing. It's like watching a thousand romances, knowing you will never fall in love. I see things. I feel things, vivid experiences that are not actually happening. They are not real, and they never will be.

My paper lay bare in front of me, a painful reminder I needed to bare myself once more. *One more story*, I thought. *One more story is all I wish to tell.* I set my pen to paper and suddenly became overwhelmed with the eerie sense I was not alone.

I turned from my desk to behold the figure of a woman, standing in the center of the room. A soft glow of light encompassed her beautiful form, and her feet hovered ever so slightly off the floor. Just as in a dream when you cannot see a person's face yet you know who they are, I could not - cannot - remember her exact detail, but I swear it looked like *her.*

"Who are you?" I asked, oddly at peace with the presence of this stranger. Then again, there was something about her that was so familiar.

The specter laughed a beautiful, musical laugh and answered in a gentle voice, "I was sent to be your guide."

The wind began to pick up, and the storm became even more violent.

"You must follow the star," she whispered, yet I heard it clear as the thoughts in my mind.

"Wait!" I called over the crashing of thunder. "What is your name? What star?"

But the room began to fade into blackness, and so did she. I felt my mind begin to slip away. Then my office, the light, and the specter were gone. There was only darkness, and I heard one word.

"Chastity."

I awoke on the ground in a dark forest, her name upon my lips.

"Chastity."

As I rolled from my stomach to my back, a groan escaped me. My vision reeled, and the world swirled around me like the white spaces of a peppermint. I looked up at the few stars watching me through the canopy of trees. *Follow the star.* I blinked and watched as the world went from still to spinning again, like the slow start of an old merry-go-round. I closed my eyes and took a deep breath before opening them again: again, the merry-go-round effect.

I could not help but laugh for a moment at the stupidity of the situation. One moment I am in my office, the next I am on the ground either drunk or sedated, looking up at the stars, reflecting on the words of a figment of my imagination. Or was she? This had to be a dream. Or maybe my office was the dream and now I had woken up.

With great effort I rolled to my side and pushed myself to my feet, leaning on a nearby tree for support. I had awoken on a gravel path encased by thick pines on either side. Both directions seemed to stretch on for miles, and my options were limited. *Forward or backward.*

I chose to move forward, or at least what I perceived as forward. I walked slowly as the ground seemed to sway beneath me, like tree tops in the wind or perhaps ships at sea. I found myself stumbling a great deal and even considered crawling on my hands and knees to ease the sensation.

It is impossible to say how long I continued on in this way. I do not recall it being long or short. I simply remember waking up, choosing a direction, and hearing the first growl.

It was not the type of growl a man will make when angry, or what comes to mind when you imagine a rabid dog. It was the type of growl a monster makes in nightmares.

I turned to look back down the path and saw a figure. Small, far off in the distance, but it was coming and it was coming fast.

I ran, or rather I tried to run. I admit I stumbled and tumbled and crashed through brush and bramble, the nightmarish creature in pursuit.

I fell through the edge of the wood and rolled down the side of a hill into a clearing. Flat on my stomach in the grass, I looked up and saw the creature that had been pursuing me. He stepped through the edge of the wood, bending a tree back as he did so.

It was a giant.

The ground trembled as he walked towards me.

Then a shadow fell over me, but not the one cast by the giant. I turned to see another figure. He wore a long black robe with his hood pulled up, his face shielded in shadow. The edges of his being seemed to move subtly, like licks of fire, dancing and disappearing into the air. He brandished a long sickle, holding it just above my fallen form, keeping the giant at bay.

"Back!" the figure demanded. His voice emanated from the faceless hollow of his hood like a mist, resonating with power.

The giant snarled but did not advance.

"You cannot take *my* life," the giant said, his voice low.

"Back," the hooded figure repeated. Each word he spoke seemed to linger.

The giant crouched low until he was sure I could see him clearly.

"Do you know who I am?" he asked.

"No," I answered.

A hideous smile twisted across his face, and his left eye rolled lazily to one side.

"Run, run, little sheep." He sang the words as if they were a lullaby and I were his child.

Fear wrapped around me like a blanket, and the giant laughed a terrible laugh. I covered my ears and hid my face in the grass. It had to be a dream. It had to stop.

Then he was gone.

Though my ears were covered I could still hear the cold, misty voice of the hooded figure when he spoke to me.

"Rise," he said.

I tried to stand but stumbled. After a moment I tried again and this time kept myself upright.

The figure turned, motioning for me to follow. He moved away from the wood and began to descend down the hill into a dark valley. The valley stretched for quite a ways but in the distance the silhouette of a city could be seen. I looked up to the sky and saw a star burning brighter than the rest. The hooded figure walked towards it.

Follow the star.

I began to follow.

As we passed deeper through the valley the air began to grow very cold. I watched as the grass died beneath my companion's robe, leaving a small trail behind us.

"You are Death," I said after some time.

The hood nodded.

"Who was the giant?" I asked.

"Great Wolf," the answer came long and drawn out.

I did not understand his answer at the time, but there was much I did not understand.

"Will he come after us?" I asked, staring at the trail of dead grass unintentionally.

I caught the end of the hood shaking *no* before he answered, "You."

I understood his meaning. *We* would not see the giant again. *I* would.

"Where are we going?" I asked.

The figure did not speak but merely pointed to the star.

"Thank you," I said. "For saving me."

He did not acknowledge this; instead, he asked only

one question.

"No fear?"

You have no fear of me is what he meant.

"This is not our first walk together," I answered.

Again he nodded, understanding.

As we walked through the valley I began to regain control of my faculties; and by the time we reached the gates of the city, I found myself feeling more lost than disoriented. I looked for a sign to learn the name of our location but could not find one. I shall simply refer to this as the nameless city. Death entered first, and I followed.

The nameless city was unlike any city I had ever seen before or have ever seen since. There stood buildings and houses, tall and ornate. It had become a melting pot of what must have been thousands of cultures all coexisting together, subtly influencing each other and yet retaining their individuality. But the most impressive part was the streets. I looked down at the shiny path beneath my feet. The roads had been somehow paved with silver. I froze for a moment in awe. Then I reached down and touched it.

"You there!" someone called.

I turned to see three figures running towards me. I wish I could describe them but indistinguishable is honestly the most accurate thing I could say. They all wore gray robes with their hoods raised, their faces covered with plain white theatre masks. The only unique characteristic about them were the tools they brought with them.

"I'm so sorry, I didn't mean to offend you by yelling," the one with the pick began.

"It's fine," I answered.

"What do you think you are doing?" the one with the shovel asked, approaching with another who carried a rake.

"No offense," he added.

"None taken," I answered, confused. "We are not from these parts," I said, motioning to Death, whom they didn't seem to care about or even notice. "Did we do something wrong?"

They looked back and forth at each other for a moment, seemingly bewildered, before the one with the pick responded.

"By the order of His Majesty the King, Tabula Rasa, no one is allowed to walk on the old roads. No offense." He stated.

"Why?" I asked.

All three of them stood silent, almost as if expectant of something, before the one with the pick answered again.

"Because they are *old*," he replied, drawing out the word the way a child might call someone a loser on the playground. "No offense."

I looked down once more at the beautiful shining silver beneath my feet.

"It doesn't look old," I stated. "In fact, it's rather beautiful."

The one with the rake gave a dramatic gasp, while the one with the shovel clutched at his heart as if struck by an arrow.

"Oh, calm down," the one with the pick said, looking at them both. "It's not from these parts, I'm sure it didn't mean any offense." He cleared his throat before turning back to me and adding, "No offense."

The one with the shovel spoke next, answering my question.

"The King said so!" he blurted out, before adding with authority, "And we...yes *we*, have been ordered to rip them up!"

He took a moment to point to their tools.

"And you... *you*!" He paused for a moment, a tone of frustration growing in his voice, "You are still using them!

You must get off!" he explained, exasperated, before adding sheepishly, "No offense."

"Where are the new roads?" I asked, and all three of them clutched at their hearts this time.

"I'm sorry!" I said. "Where should I walk?"

The three of them pointed in unison in the direction from which they had come from.

"You will find the end of the road in *that* direction," the one with the pick said. "The King has decided we no longer require roads in this city. I suggest you stop thinking of them altogether. No offense."

I thanked them for their time and began walking in the direction they had pointed me. As I came to the end of the road, I saw that it did not simply end but that it had been shattered and the ground scraped raw. Almost half a foot down there lay nothing but dirt. The crew had been careful to remove even the tiniest of fragments of the silver road. A wheelbarrow to my left had been loaded with the pieces for disposal.

As I stepped off of the silver and down into the dirt I heard a sudden small applause. I turned to see the three masked figures watching and clapping for me. Then the one with the pick turned to his companions and said, "Alright, back to work, no offense!" and they continued to tear up the roads.

Death and I continued on along the dirt paths. It saddened me to see the silver road was not the only thing being uprooted. As we journeyed deeper through the city I noticed that the buildings became simpler, very tall and completely stone. They looked like the skyscrapers in our cities but less unattractive. I noticed several of the cloaked figures working to remove a statue, while still more were decommissioning and removing a fountain. I assume someday the whole city will suffer a similar fate to that of the roads.

The people of the city were neither rude nor polite. All were cloaked and masked. I saw no men or women, no children nor old, only the indistinct figures that resembled people. No one spoke to me nor I to them. I followed close behind Death as he moved through the city with a perfected precision, not touching anyone.

We came upon a port at what I assume was the far end of the city. It reached out into the waters of a river, not a small wooden dock, but a large stone port for freight ships. Many merchants had set up shop there, and it had become somewhat of a small marketplace. This confused me as I realized the port was empty of freighters or even small merchant vessels. In fact, not a single ship had docked there, or so I thought. Death led me to a small black skiff, it rode so low on the water it could barely be seen.

Many turned to watch as I boarded after Death. Emotionless, eyeless masks turned in my direction. Death pushed us out into the river, using the staff of his sickle against the stone and then the water. I watched as the city faded into the distance, and for some time we were alone.

I was eighteen when I first encountered Death. He came and took my mother from me which, as you can imagine, left a lasting impression. When the smoke and mirrors are taken away from the show of life, and the illusion of immortality is broken, we are left with the haunting question everybody asks and only few can answer: what does it all mean? And a clock, or rather, a time bomb, in your mind begins to tick.

I think that is why some people write, to create something to leave behind. To show they were here and, possibly, even that they mattered. That is one of the many beauties of stories. They can reach across time and resonate with others.

I was once on a date with a young woman who had read a fraction of my work. She asked me what I like to write about and I surprised myself when I instinctively answered, "pain." Pain is relatable, universal. Just like death, it surpasses race, religion, and sex. It unites people and also divides them beyond repair.

The truth is I really don't wish to write about pain, but rather I want to write about hope. Pain is just the medium. Pain is the dark etchings of a charcoal drawing, and hope is the blank spaces that add a sense of context. They reach out to the viewer and complete the picture.

I would like to say my journey down the river with Death was a pleasant trip, but the truth is it was not. Death stood behind me, polling the boat with the rod of his sickle. I watched the forests on either side of us. It felt as though we were moving through a tunnel as the trees rose overhead and reached in towards us. I found looking in the water to be much more interesting. There I saw hundreds of people looking back at me. At first, I believed that they were perhaps criminals who had been drowned, but they moved beneath the surface as though they still had life. One of them looked up at me as we glided by on the surface. They all wore decorated masks. As we moved further along the river, the masks grew plainer, and eventually, there were no masks at all. There were men and women, old and young, children in the river, all of them seemingly unaware of their location.

"Memories," I heard Death murmur behind me.

Fear smothered me as I realized what he meant. These were the memories of those who had traveled down this river before me. Starting with the most recent and returning generations, the further we travelled. Hundreds if not thousands of life journeys that had been lived now rested here, washed away from the minds of their owners.

"Will I forget too?" I asked, not taking my eyes off of

the beautiful images beneath me. They flickered and swayed with the light current of the water, yet their motions were deliberate. I began to feel a bit like I was watching an old movie on an old television, the picture slightly obscured and the color only a little less vibrant than the real world.

I looked to Death when I heard no answer. The hood shook slowly back and forth. *No.* I would remember. Though now I wish I had forgotten. My gaze returned to the waters and I was stunned to find I recognized one of the people beneath the surface.

"Mother!" I cried, but she did not hear.

My hands plunged through the waters, reaching for her, but they grasped nothing. A small sliver of pain entered me as if I had been stung by a bee on the tip of each finger.

"Mother!" I yelled again, reaching deeper this time. The boat rocked and the waves splashed against my chest. I slid further and further out of the skiff. I could see her, and we were closer now. I reached for her a total of three times, but each time I was met with empty arms. The pain deepened and moved through my fingers, across my hands, and up into my chest. It felt like electricity, energizing and incinerating.

Hot tears burned down my face, not from the pain in my arms but from the pain of the memories. I called to her once more, and for a moment she turned as if she had heard me, but that would have been impossible. The staff of Death's sickle scooped under me, crossing my chest, and pulled me violently back into the boat.

"No!" he commanded, pointing the blunt end of his tool at my weeping form. I lay on the floor of the boat, memories now flooding my mind.

The pain in my arms did not subside until we were almost all the way down the river.

Once it did, I found myself listening to the rod of the sickle cutting gently through the water again. Death propelled the craft gracefully through the waters. We did not speak, nor did I look back into the river.

When the boat stopped, I stepped out onto a small stone pier which connected to something I can only describe as an enchanted city. A light fog crept off of the water, but the port was illuminated by the glow of thousands of tiny fireflies. I looked back when I noticed Death had not followed.

"Are you coming?" I asked.

The hood shook.

"How will I know the way?"

He pointed up at the night sky, and I realized what he meant. The star which shone brighter than the rest hung almost directly above me now. I turned back towards Death and watched as he piloted the craft back the way we had come. The trees and the fog over the still water slowly swallowed the black hooded figure.

"Thank you," I whispered, somehow certain he heard me.

I turned to the city gates that stood before me. The phrase, *"The unexamined life is not worth living,"* had been carved into the archway.

"Aristotle," I whispered.

"Socrates, actually," I heard Chastity say as she appeared at my side, her feet hovering just above the cobblestone.

"Chastity, where have you been?" I asked.

"Where you had to go I am not permitted to enter," she said. "But I am with you now, and with you I shall remain."

"Where are we?" I asked.

"The City of Fallen Heroes," she answered, gesturing in the direction of the gates. We walked together, or rather I walked and she floated into the city.

The City of Fallen Heroes looked just as you would expect. It was an ancient stone city, that had begun to be overtaken by flowers, vines, and vegetation, and could have been mistaken for a mythical garden. There were pillars and archways and steps that led to nowhere, or rather, had once led somewhere but no longer did. But the most captivating part were the statues.

As if frozen in stone thousands of years ago, there stood hundreds upon hundreds of statues. I saw many I recognized and many more I did not. There was a Roman man standing on a bridge, a young boy in full Spartan battle gear, and a man on a cross.

The truth is I always wanted to be a hero. I grew up reading countless tales of ancient myths and hundreds of comics with masked vigilantes. As I grew older I found they were just that: stories. Tools to teach children ideals. No one actually wore a mask and a cape while making a final stand for humanity. No, we grow up and we realize the world is more complex than children's books, and we learn to become complex with it.

As we walked through this graveyard of history, I found Chastity's presence quite comforting. Death had been a rather silent companion, and Chastity was as well. But there was something about the soft glow which emanated from her that seemed warm and peaceful. She stopped as we came to a new section of the city, where the statues had been lined like a standing army awaiting their orders.

"Who are they?" I asked.

"They are the unrecognized," Chastity answered. "Fathers and mothers, friends, and strangers. It would take decades to tell all of their stories."

I remembered I had once worked in an office and someone very high up in the company was coming to visit. I was told to have a question prepared for him. When the time came I asked him, "Who are your heroes?" The question reduced the man to tears. He told me he had recently lost both of his parents; that they had been his heroes.

Heroism is not unattainable, it's just not always glamorous. Most of it is probably the internal struggle to stand by those ideals you were taught as a child: when you remove the veil of complexity from the world, and from yourself, and remember how simple it can be: right and wrong. I looked over the lines of statues, deeply moved, when an overwhelming desire to leave struck me. I felt common and out of place.

"Come, we must go," Chastity said.

We continued through the city, stopping here and there as I examined some of the statues and asked Chastity questions. The real answers of this journey did not come though, until we came upon the tower.

Somewhere in the city a tower stands reaching, not just to the sky but to the star that shines brighter than the rest. When we came upon it, I walked to the door at its base and lifted the latch. To my surprise, the door opened. I stepped inside and began to ascend the spiral stairs. Chastity did not follow.

As I came to the last steps, I could see there was a room at the top of the tower. I entered as if out of the floor and stepped into the odd octagonal room, which had walls made of mirrors. It terrified me at first, as I did not see my reflection in any of them.

"You have arrived," I heard above me, and looked up to see Chastity reappear in the cone-shaped ceiling space just above the walls. She descended until her feet were just above the mirrors.

"Where am I?" I asked her.

"Where you need to be," she answered with a smile.

The low rumbling of a growl caught my ears, and my eyes returned to the mirrors. I saw myself for the first time, and behind me I saw a wolf.

This was not an ordinary wolf. It was old, sick, and evil.

I spun around to defend myself and found myself face to face with the giant. He had caught up to me. Behind the giant in the mirror I saw no giant but rather the wolf I had seen before.

"What is this place?" I asked, my gaze moving from the giant to Chastity.

"Do not be afraid," she said. "The giant before you is merely what he wants you to see. The mirror will show you what really is."

I looked back at the sickly creature in the mirror and then to the giant before me. Afraid, I turned my back to the giant, facing him in the mirror, feeling the room I saw in the mirror was more real than the room I was standing in.

"Now it's your turn," I said, looking up to Chastity.

"That is not how it works. But that you may understand..."

She descended only enough for the very tips of her toes to reflect in the mirror, and a blinding light, brighter than the sun, drove me to my knees. The wolf behind me yelped in pain. The light faded as Chastity returned to her place above us.

A deep silence followed, and in the silence I realized why I was here. A sense of awe fell over me at the realization I had to look into the mirrors, not to see the wolf or Chastity, but to see me. A deep fear rose at the thought. Her beauty had been blinding. What hideous shape would I see of myself?

I felt the hair on the back of my neck begin to stand on end before realizing it was not my hair but fur gently brushing against me.

"You don't have to," the wolf whispered. "Come with me, and I will keep you safe."

For a second I did feel safe. The consoling touch of the soft fur soothed me. I could leave and never return. I would never have to face the mirror again.

"No," I whispered. I stared into the mirror, looking

deep. At first I saw nothing. Then an image began to form. It was the image of a tired old man. He clutched a painting close to his heart. It depicted a woman of incredible beauty.

I turned to the second mirrored wall and saw a creature with long black hair hung around a pale face with deep pained eyes almost as dark as a night sky. His scaled hands were tipped with sharp nails more like claws.

In the third mirror, I saw a hybrid between a wolf and a man.

In the fourth stood a coward before an empty throne.

The fifth revealed a man with a tattoo on his arm. It depicted a sword planted in the ground, a cape and helmet resting on top.

The sixth mirror showed a young man in robes holding dark magic in one hand and a strong light, like a flare, in the other.

In the seventh stood an actor who clawed at his face, trying to remove a mask.

In the eighth and last mirror, I saw myself.

A priest once told me to write letters to *her* but not to send them, and so I did. It helped, and eventually, I stopped writing to *her*, but I never stopped writing. A door had been thrown open and a spring breeze had swept through the house, stirring up the dust and cutting through the sickening scent of depression and decay. I began to write frequently, story after story, trying to cope with more than just *her*. I wrote to cope with *myself.*

People imagine the soul as an unseen heart, something which can be broken and crushed, but they are wrong. The soul is like blood. It moves through everything and gives life. It can bleed, and I have bled into my work.

The Artist, Jude, Daniel, Silas, Alexander, David, Matthias... I looked at them all, remembering every accident, mistake, cruel intention, and moment of surrender, every pain, and every time I rose to something greater. Every instance that inspired and shaped them into the creations they had become. Tiny mirrors of my sins and my successes. The hero and the villain. The man and the monster.

This is it, I thought, staring into the mirrors. *This is where man and monster meet.*

I looked to each of them one last time as they faded, and all that was left was myself.

I do not know how long I had been sitting at my desk. I do not remember returning to my office or opening my eyes. I was just suddenly there again, staring blankly into my paper. I looked around, half expecting to see Chastity or the wolf, but they were both gone. I caught my own reflection in the glass cover of a picture that sits on my desk. I stared at it for a moment, remembering. Then I picked up my pen and began to write.

The truth is...

About the Author

Eric Tamburino is an American author of short fairy tales. In early school years, he struggled particularly with reading but always found it easier to learn when information was presented in story form. He graduated with a bachelor's degree in communications and works as a marketing specialist. He hopes to work in film someday. He loves storytelling and continues to write, both to entertain and to teach.

Contact:
wheremanandmonstermeet@gmail.com
https://wheremanandmonstermeet.com

Acknowledgments

I would like to say thank you to a great many people who assisted me in the completion in this book, some of whom include: Loretta C., Sarah L., Emma J., Tom P., Luke S., Chris L., my wife, and of course my father, mother, and sister. There are too many more to list here but please know that I am grateful.

Thank you for the discussions, the editing, for believing in me, and for reminding me that this was worth doing.

36848535R00137

Made in the USA
Middletown, DE
19 February 2019